Alfred Bate Richards

A Short Sketch of the Career of Capt. Richard F. Burton

Alfred Bate Richards

A Short Sketch of the Career of Capt. Richard F. Burton

ISBN/EAN: 9783337013622

Printed in Europe, USA, Canada, Australia, Japan

Cover: Foto ©Raphael Reischuk / pixelio.de

More available books at **www.hansebooks.com**

A Short Sketch of the Career

OF

Captain Richard F. Burton

COLLECTED FROM "MEN OF EMINENCE;" FROM CAPTAIN AND
MRS. BURTON'S OWN WORKS; FROM THE PRESS, FROM
PERSONAL KNOWLEDGE, AND VARIOUS
OTHER RELIABLE SOURCES

BY

AN OLD OXONIAN

WHO IS PROUD TO CLAIM HIM AS AN OXFORD MAN AND AS AN
OLD FRIEND

WILLIAM MULLAN AND SON
LONDON AND BELFAST
1880

A SHORT SKETCH OF THE CAREER

OF

CAPTAIN RICHARD F. BURTON.

In the foremost rank of the noble band of illustrious explorers of which England is so justly proud, stands Captain Richard Francis Burton, late of Her Majesty's Bombay Army (18th Native Infantry); Chief of Staff Irregular Cavalry serving in the Crimea; Her Britannic Majesty's Consul for the West Coast of Africa; for Santos (São Paulo, Brazil); for Damascus, and now for Trieste, Austria, the celebrated Eastern traveller, author, and linguist, and gold medallist of the English and French Royal Geographical Societies.

Richard Burton's grandfather was the Rev. Edward Burton, Rector of Tuam in Galway (who with his brother, Bishop Burton, of Tuam, were the first of this branch to settle in Ireland). They were two of the Burtons of Barker Hill, near Shap, Westmoreland, who own a common ancestor with the Burtons of Yorkshire, of Carlow, and Northamptonshire. Richard Burton's grandfather married Maria Margaretta Campbell, daughter, by a Lejeune, of Dr. John Campbell, LL.D., Vicar-General of Tuam. Their son was Richard Burton's father, Lieut.-Colonel Joseph Netterville Burton, of the 36th Regiment, who married a Miss (Beckwith) Baker, of Nottinghamshire, a descendant, on her mother's side,

B

of the Scotch Macgregors. The Lejeune above mentioned was related to the Montmorencys and Drelincourts, French Huguenots of the time of Louis XIV. (See Appendix A.) To this hangs a story which will be told by-and-bye. This Lejeune, whose real name was Louis Lejeune, is supposed to have been a son of Louis XIV. by the Huguenot Countess of Montmorency. He was secretly carried off to Ireland. His name was translated to Louis Young, and he eventually became a Doctor of Divinity. The Royal, or rather Morganatic, marriage contract was asserted to have existed, but has disappeared. The Lady Primrose, who, according to the various documents, either brought him to Ireland, or married him after she became a widow, was buried, by her own desire, with an iron casket in her hands, and it is supposed that some State secret, or papers, may have been concealed in this way.

Richard Francis Burton was born on the 19th March, 1821, at Barham House, Herts.

His education as a traveller and linguist commenced in his fifth year, when he was taken to the Continent. Here, with the exception of a few months passed at the Rev. Mr. Delafosse's school (Richmond, Surrey), he continued, until the age of nineteen, travelling through France, Switzerland, Germany, and Italy, and thus acquiring a practical knowledge of modern European languages and fencing.

In 1840 he entered Trinity College, Oxford, where he remained until 1842. This is a curious reflection at school for any boy or any master, " What *will* become of the boy? Who will turn out well, who ill, who will distinguish himself, who remain in obscurity, who live, who die ?" I am sure, although Burton was brilliant, rather wild, and very popular, none of us foresaw his future greatness, nor knew what a treasure we had amongst us. His studies hitherto, whether abroad or at home, had been directed towards the Church. A commission in the Indian army having, however, been offered him, he accepted it; and, presently, he found himself, at the age of twenty-one, in Bombay, posted to the 18th Bombay Native Infantry, then at Baroda, Guzerat, towards the close of the Afghan war.

Within the first year of his Indian sojourn, he had passed examinations in Hindostanee and Guzeratee.

At a somewhat later period this indefatigable scholar and soldier proved his proficiency in five other Oriental languages—Persian, Maharattee, Sindhee, Punjaubee, and Arabic; had attacked Telugu and Pushtu (the Afghan tongue), and was studying literary and conversational Turkish and Armenian.

In 1844 Lieutenant Burton proceeded to Sind with the 18th Native Infantry, and was immediately placed, under Colonel Walter Scott, upon the Staff of Sir Charles Napier, who soon discovered his merits, and turned them to account. With the exception of a visit to Goa and the Neilgherries—the visit which gave rise to Lieutenant Burton's first volume entitled "Goa and the Blue Mountains"—the five following years were spent by him in the Sind Canal Survey, and in collecting materials for his "Sindh, or the Races that inhabit the Valley of the Indus;" "Scinde, or the Unhappy Valley;" and "Falconry in the Valley of the Indus."

With a view for employment on active service in Mooltan, he had, in 1849, published in the Journal of the Bombay Asiatic Society, "Notes on the Pushtu, Jan. 7, 1849," and a "Grammar on the Játaki or Belochkí Dialect." He joined his regiment when marching upon Mooltan to attack the Sikhs.

Part of his training had been uncommonly good and rare. While on the survey he received frequent permission to travel amongst the wild tribes of the hills and plains to collect information for Sir Charles Napier. He used to exchange his European dress or uniform for the tattered robes of a Dervish, and, bidding adieu to civilisation, wander about the country on foot, lodging in Mosques and with the strangest company. Thus he became well acquainted with the Beloch and Brahui tribes, those Indo-Sythians who were then so little known. His chief danger was that the people insisted on his being a saint, and when a village wants a patron it is uncommonly fond of putting to death some holy pilgrim with all the honours, and using his tomb as a place to pray at. The metamorphose was so complete that not only natives but even Europeans never suspected it; and on one occasion he rode a dromedary from the Gateway of Hyderabad, meeting his Colonel face to face, who never imagined for a moment it was Burton. From these excursions he used to return with a rich budget of news and information, which proved not a little useful to the local Government. During his surveying excursions, whilst levelling down the canals, he also worked in native dress, and thus he arrived at secrets which were quite out of the reach of his brother officers and surveyors. Hence Captain, now General Macmurdo, frequently consulted his journals, and the Survey books were highly praised by the Surveyor-General.

Eventually, after seven years of this kind of life, over-work and over-study, combined with the "hot season" and the march up the Indus Valley caused some suffering to our gallant and erudite young soldier, and, at the end of the campaign, he was attacked by severe ophthalmia, the result of mental and physica over-fatigue;—thus he was compelled by sickness to return to Europe, *viâ* the Cape.

Residing principally in France upon his return, he was there awarded the *Brevet de Pointe* for the excellence of his swordsmanship. It has been observed of Captain Burton, that as horseman, swordsman, and marksman, no soldier of his day could surpass, and few equalled him. In 1853 he published a System of Bayonet Exercise (Clowes, London), which, although undervalued at the time, has since been made use of by the Horse Guards.*

Even the late Colonel Sykes, who was Burton's friend, sent for him and sharply reproached him with printing a book which would do far more harm than good. All the old Waterloo officers seemed to fancy that bayonet exercise would make the men unsteady in the ranks, so that official " wigging" was the principal award Burton got. And yet every European nation, not to speak of the American army, was at the time engaged in perfecting its bayonet exercise. Thus, a few years afterwards, the much-abused pamphlet was liberally used by the Horse Guards, in order to form an official system. One day the author received an immense letter from the Treasury, with a seal the size of a baby's fist. He opened it, with high expectations, and found, not a compliment nor a word o thanks, the only thing he would have valued, but gracious permission to draw one shilling. This is the usual custom when military authorities borrow from professional works by officers on full pay, and then there is no infringement of authors' rights. Poor Captain Blakeley, the inventor of Blakeley's guns, calculated his losses in

---

* This little Manual, which has its history, I will reproduce at the end of the Christmas number of this book, that boys intended for military service may interest themselves in it, and practice their drill if they like, and also Burton's sword exercise.

this way at several hundred thousands of pounds. However, Burton was not a loser, except in time and disappointment. He went to the War Office and was sent to half a dozen different rooms, to the intense astonishment of us many clerks, and after three-quarters of an hour's hard work, succeeded in drawing his shilling, which he gave to the first beggar.

Nearly a century and a half ago Marshal Saxe, of famous memory, called the gun the musket-handle. Alexandre Dumas declared it an act of patriotism to teach Governments the resources of this weapon ; and he justly remarks that, as the sword decided individual, so the bayonet settles national questions. It is curious to remark that every nation prides itself on its own peculiar prowess with the bayonet. According to their own respective writers the weapon in which the English excel the French, and the French the English, both of them the Germans, and the Germans both of them, is the bayonet.

In April, 1853, supported by the Royal Geographical Society, Richard Burton prepared to penetrate into Arabia under circumstances unusually strange, and peculiarly well adapted to facilitate his object in view— study of "the inner life of the Moslem." With this expedition opens the most romantic chapter in the history of this remarkable man.

He had long felt within himself the qualifications, mental and physical, which are needed for the exploration of dangerous regions, difficult of access. Not alone had his previous education and his career as a Dervish in Sind especially prepared him for such enterprises ; but with a mind, at once practical and imaginative, grasping every contingency likely to arise, he had sought to accomplish himself thoroughly for this mission in the

most trifling as well as in the most important directions.
Thus it is related that he took lessons from a blacksmith
in order not only, in case of need, to shoe his horse, but
also to make its shoes.

For penetrating with safety into Arabia, it was necessary that our traveller should be absolutely unknown;
indeed, he appears to have assumed and sustained
various Oriental characters. He left London as a
Persian, and travelled to Southampton with a friend,
Captain Grindlay kindly acting as his interpreter.
Landing at Alexandria, he was received in the house of
the excellent John Thurburn who, curious to say, was
the host of Burckhardt till the Swiss traveller died. He
and his son-in-law, John Larking, now of the Firs, Lee,
Kent—were the only persons throughout Richard Burton's perilous expedition who knew his secret. To Cairo
he went as a Dervish, living there as a native until the
time of the departure of the Pilgrims. Unable, as he
had intended, to cross Arabia on account of the disturbances caused by the Russian war, he performed the
pilgrimage described in his work, published in 1855,
entitled "Pilgrimage to Meccah and Medinah."*
The peculiarity of this pilgrimage consists in the Holy
City having been visited by this bold and subtle Englishman as one of "the Faithful." As converted Moslems,
many Europeans have of late gone there. They have been
received with the utmost civility consistent with coldness,
have been admitted to outward friendship, but have been
carefully kept out of what they most wished to know and
see, so that Burton was thus the first European who had

---

* 3 vols., Longmans; 2nd edition, 1857. Translated in the "Revue
des deux Mondes;" republished by Putnam & Co., New York. Cheap
edition, William Mullan & Son, 1879.

beheld the inner and religious life of the Moslem as one of themselves.

There is a story (amongst many others) current about Burton, viz., that two men watching some of his habits, suspected him of not being a Mohometan, and, that he perceiving it, shot them both to avoid detection. Nobody enjoys these grim jokes against himself so much as Burton, who little recks what impression they may produce upon small minds who are unused to danger, but the fact is, this is not true. Nobody ever doubted his origin, and therefore, he had no need to defend himself, and it should be contradicted.

We have said that various were the Oriental characters assumed by this explorer of versatile genius. The one easiest sustained appears to have been that of half-Arab half-Iranian, whose brethren throng the northern shores of the Persian Gulf. With hair falling on his shoulders, long beard, his face, hands, arms, and legs stained with a thin coat of henna, Oriental dress, spear in hand, pistols in belt, such was Richard Burton, *alias* Mirza Abdullah, el-Bushiri, as he commenced his adventurous life; the explorer who has since been from north to south, from east to west, and mixed with all nations and tribes, without betraying himself in manners, customs, or speech, often when death must have ensued had he created either suspicion or dislike.

Richard Burton's talents for mixing with and assimilating natives of all countries, but especially Oriental characters, and of becoming as one of themselves without any one doubting or suspecting his origin; his perfect knowledge of their languages, manners, customs, habits, and religion ; and last, but not least, his being gifted by nature with an Arab head and face, favoured this his first great enterprise. One can learn from that versatile poet-traveller, the excellent Théophile Gautier, why Richard Burton is an Arab in appearance; and account for that incurable restlessness that is unable to wrest from fortune a spot on earth wherein to repose when weary of wandering like the Desert sands.

"There is a reason," says Gautier, who had studied the Andalusian and the Moor, "for that fantasy of nature which causes an Arab to be born in Paris, or a Greek in Auvergne ; the mysterious voice of blood which is silent for generations, or only utters a confused murmur, speaks at rare intervals a more intelligible language. In the general confusion race claims its own, and some forgotten ancestor asserts his rights. Who knows what alien drops are mingled with our blood? The great migrations from the tablelands of India, the descents of the Northern races, the Roman and Arab invasions, have all left their marks. Instincts which seem *bizarre* spring from these confused recollections, these hints of a distant country. The vague desire of this primitive Fatherland moves such minds as retain the more vivid memories of the past. Hence the wild unrest that wakens in certain spirits the need of flight, such as the cranes and the swallows feel when kept in bondage—the impulses that make a man leave his luxurious life to bury himself in the Steppes, the Desert, the Pampas, the Sáhara. He goes to seek his brothers. It would be easy to point out the intellectual Fatherland of our greatest minds. Lamartine, De Musset, and De Vigny, are English ; Delacroix is an Anglo-Indian : Victor Hugo a Spaniard; Ingres belongs to the Italy of Florence and Rome.

Richard Burton has also some peculiarities which oblige one to suspect a drop of Oriental, perhaps Gypsy, blood. By Gypsy we must understand the pure Eastern race, not the tramps called "Gipsies" in England. There are but few remnants of these unmixed families in Europe with English names—one of which is Burton. They have a peculiar eye. When it looks at you, it looks through you, and then glazing over, seems to see something behind you. Richard Burton is the only man (not a Gypsy) with that peculiarity, and he shows, with them, the same horror of a corpse, death-bed scenes, and graveyards, though caring but little for his own life.

Returning to Egypt for a few months, he proceeded to Bombay; and, assisted by the late Lord Elphinstone, then Governor of Western India, organized an expedition into Somali-land, East Africa, taking Lieutenant, afterwards *the* Captain, Speke as second in command, and two Indian officers, Lieutenants Stroyan, I N., and Herne, Bo. N.I. The object was to visit Harar, in Moslem Abysinnia, the Timbuctoo of East Africa, the exploration of which had in vain been attempted by some thirty travellers. Disguised as an Arab, he was successful; and returned to Aden with the first authentic notices of this mysterious City, the southernmost masonry-built settlement in North Equatorial Africa. Terrible sufferings in the Desert had been endured on the way from want of water and food—sufferings almost unto death.

The Somali Expedition terminated disastrously. The explorers were attacked in the night at Berberah by the natives, who endeavoured to throw down their tents, and catch them, as it were, in a trap. All four fought bravely against overpowering numbers. Burton and Speke were both desperately wounded. Poor Stroyan was killed, whilst Herne was untouched, though he followed his leader, cutting his way valiantly through the enemy.

Captain Speke had eleven wounds, and Captain Burton, with a lance transfixing his jaws and palate, wandered up and down the coast, suffering from wounds, hunger and thirst. They met; left the natives to sack their property; but, carrying off the dead body of their comrade, they were at last picked up by a native dhow, or boat.

The severe nature of Lieutenant Burton's wounds compelled his return to England. Having read an account of his explorations before the Royal Geographical Society, and published " First Footsteps in East Africa,"* he again left his native land, this time bound for the Crimea, and landed at Balaklava.

In the Crimea he was employed as Chief of the Staff of Irregular Cavalry, of which indeed he was the principal organizer; and, at the moment of their disbanding, 4000 sabres were in perfect training, ready to do anything and to go anywhere. He also, by the order of General Beatson, volunteered to Lord Stratford de Redcliffe to convoy any amount of provision for the relief of Kars. But Kars was already doomed, and the offer only excited official wrath. It was the terrible mistake of over-zeal. General Beatson and his Staff were compelled, by complication of small intrigues, to resign, and the subject of this memoir returned to England. Lord Palmerston was going to send Captain Burton to raise a large body of Kurdish Horse to attack Georgia and aid Circassia, when peace was proclaimed.

When Captain Burton was at Constantinople Lord Stratford de Redcliffe, whose fervent disciple and great admirer Burton was, had set his heart upon personally communicating, by a trusty messenger, with Schamyl, of patriotic fame. Accordingly, Lord Napier and Ettrick was

* Longmans, 1856; the Appendix, containing a Grammar of the Harar Dialect. This work was translated into French by a Belgian publisher.

commissioned to sound Burton about a secret expedition to the Moslem's Head-quarters. He was delighted with the prospect, and laid before them his plans, and showed them where obstacles would have to be encountered, that he might be empowered to deal with them. He told them that Schamyl, made suspicious by constant treachery, would first ask him, as an Envoy of the Great Eltchi, what terms, or how many guns and thousand pounds sterling he had brought him, or was to bring him. Had the answer been "Nothing," the visit would have been deemed one of simple curiosity and the visitor a "spy," in which case nothing could have saved his life. For this end he would have had, moreover, to ride through some 300 miles of Russian territory. He would, however, have thought but little of this danger and difficulty, and he would, beforehand, have arranged to be assisted to the utmost by the patriotic Circassians; and such an expedition would have had the protection of all the harems of Constantinople. However, the Great Eltchi, the greatest Eastern Diplomatist we have ever had or shall ever have, did not think the affair justified the risks, and refused to offer any definite terms, without which the enterprise would have been utterly useless, so it fell to the ground.

At the instance of the Royal Geographical Society, Lord Clarendon, Secretary of State for Foreign Affairs, supplied Captain Burton with funds for an exploration of the then utterly unknown Lake Region of Central Africa. In October, 1856, he set out for Bombay, accompanied, as second in command, by his former companion, Captain Speke, and landed at Zanzibar on December 19th, 1856. Energetically assisted by the late Lieutenant-Colonel Hamerton, Her Majesty's Consul at Zanzibar, the explorers made a tentative expedidition, between the 5th January, 1857, and March 6th, 1857, to the regions about Mombas. Struck down, however, by the dangerous remittent known as "Coast fever," they were forced to return to their head-quarters at Zanzibar.

After a prolonged re-organization, our dauntless explorers, Burton and Speke, set forth, once more, bound for the regions of the far interior, into which only one European, M. Maizan, a French naval officer, had attempted to penetrate,—he having been cruelly murdered at the very commencement of his journey. The result of this memorable expedition, which occupied the years from 1856 to 1859, is well known to the world through Captain Burton's work.* It was the base upon which all subsequent journeys were founded. The lamented Livingstone, the gallant Cameron, and the adventurous Stanley have carried it out. Now, where the explorers found the rudest barbarians, two church missions have been established, and a railway is proposed to connect the Coast with the Lake regions.¯ This expedition brought neither honour nor profit to Burton; but the world is not likely to forget it. The Future will probably be juster and more generous than the Past or Present.

During these African explorations Captain Burton felt severely the effects of the climate, being attacked by fever twenty-one times, and having suffered temporarily from paralysis and partial blindness.

In May, 1859, this brave traveller returned to England, where he immediately proposed another expedition

* "The Lake Regions of Equatorial Africa,'' and through the volume of the Journal of the Royal Geographical Society for 1860. The former was translated into French by Madame H. Loreau, and republished in New York by Harper, 1861.

to the sources of the Nile. The Royal Geographical Society did not, however, encourage the proposal.

In April, 1860, Captain Burton set out for the United States, and, passing through the country of the Mormons, visited California. He returned to England in December, 1860, having spent six weeks with Brigham Young, the Prophet, at Great Salt Lake City, and travelled during his American expedition twenty-five thousand miles. In California he visited the gold-diggings, and learnt practically to use pick and pan. The experiences of this journey were given forth in a work entitled " The City of the Saints."*

In 1861, when the Indian army changed hands, Captain Burton suffered. He had accepted from Earl Russell the Consulship of Fernando Po. When the Indian army became the Queen's army, Indian officers enjoyed the same privileges as the Queen's officers. In the old days an Indian officer could not have held an appointment in Africa and remain on half-pay; but with the new arrangements they could, as there were many cases on record of officers being allowed to take appointments and remain on the cadre of the Staff-Corps of India. I do not quote names, but any man who knows Egypt can score off half-a-dozen. However, Burton had been too free with his remarks upon the political neglect of the Court of Directors, and other *láches* on the shores of the Red Sea, which, had he been listened to, would have prevented the Jeddah massacre. He was too young an " official" to be listened to; his interference was disliked, and when an opportunity came for getting rid of him—though it would have been stretching no poin*, to have granted this appointment and being retained in the

* Longmans, 1861. It was reprinted by Messrs. Harper, of New York; and extensively reviewed by the " Tour du Monde."

army on half pay—it was refused, and they swept out his
whole nineteen years' service as if they had never been,
without a vestige of pay or pension. He realised only,
on seeing his successor gazetted, that his military career
was ended, and that his past life was become like a blank
sheet of paper.

The old proverb, "When God shuts one door, He
opens another," seemed to come to pass. Captain
Burton married this year (1861) into one of the most
ancient Catholic families in England, his wife being
Isabel, daughter of Henry Raymond Arundell (*vide* the
ninth Lord Arundell of Wardour),* by Eliza, sister of

* Lord Arundell of Wardour, between 1580 and 1595, fought with
Rodolph of Hapsburg against the Turks, and at the siege of Gran,
in Hungary, took the Turkish standard with his own hands. In all
these battles he is represented as a knight in black armour, perform-
ing prodigies of valour. Lord Arundell had borne with him a letter
from Queen Elizabeth of England, dated from Westminster Palace,
February 10, 1579, commending him to the care and notice of the
Emperor Rodolph of Hapsburg, wherein she styles him as "our
beloved kinsman, a youth well instructed in the best letters, who is
travelling to collect knowledge and to learn the manners of Noble
Provinces." The Queen, in terming Thomas Lord Arundell, "con-
sanguineus noster predilectus," and "adolescentum nobis sanguinea
propinquitate conjunctum," had several connections to choose from,
for he was closely allied to her both by blood and marriage, but she,
perhaps, alluded to the marriage of the first Sir Thomas Arundell
with his cousin, the sister of Queen Katharine Howard (*ride* Duke
of Norfolk), and to his mother having been Lady Eleanor Grey,
daughter of the Marquis of Dorset, and also to Thomas Lord Arundell's own mother having been Margaret Willoughby, whose mother
was sister to Henry Grey, Duke of Suffolk, husband of Mary, Queen
Dowager of France and sister to Henry the 8th. The Emperor,
delighted with Arundell's brave and gallant conduct and bearing,
loaded him with honours, and created him, on the field of battle, a
Count of the Sacred Roman Empire, with all the rank and privileges
of an Austrian noble, to descend to his legitimate posterity, male and
female, for ever. Hence, every legitimately born Arundell is a Count
or Countess of the Great German Empire of Rodolph of Hapsburg,

the present Lord Gerard, of Garswood, Lancashire. His wife, who was brought up at the Convent of the Holy Sepulchre in England, has for the last nineteen years been his faithful companion, entering into all his pursuits like a man, and serving him as Secretary and aide-de-camp.

Shortly after his marriage, Captain Burton went to the Consulship of Fernando Po, in the Bight of Biafra, on the West Coast of Africa. The whole Bight, 600 miles and the title and privileges and traditions are still kept up in Austria, where Mrs. Burton ranks as Countess. In England, when a title is conferred, the head of the family alone takes it, whereas in Austria, and in most other countries, it is assumed by the whole family; in the case of a woman marrying into another family, she retains her title, but it dies with her, and does not extend to her husband or her children. A British subject does not assume a foreign title in England without the express leave of the Sovereign.

This family of Arundell of Wardour is a race to whom the Conquest seems almost a modern date. They live in their old Castle of Wardour in almost patriarchal simplicity, pure in their Tory-Conservatism, staunch Royalists and Catholics, standing aloof from the world's rush, contrary to the wont of their ancestors, a long line of brave men and chaste women, whose deeds fill pages of history, whose marriages were princely, as shown by several Royal descents, and by one hundred and four unbroken quarterings. And as those know who have free access to the gloomy chests of archives containing musty, worm eaten documents, they are the most ancient family in the kingdom, and the nearest allied to Royalty in England. They are the real Earls of Arundel, and head of that ancient family, and are, as such, entitled to be the Lords of Buckenham, the Premier Barony of the kingdom, from William Albini, First Earl of Arundel, by Queen Adeliza, widow of Henry I., who traces her pedigree direct back to Charlemagne. They have also a Royal descent from the Hapsburgs of Austria. ' The Arundel women are likewise hereditary Canonesses of the Holy Sepulchre.

Sir John Arundell, of Lanherne, father of Sir Thomas Arundell, of Wardour Castle, married Lady Eleanor Grey, daughter of the Marquis of Dorset, whose mother was Elizabeth Wydeville, daughter of Sir Richard Wydeville, Earl of Rivers (extinct), who married Jacqueline of Luxembourg (daughter of the Earl of St. Paul) who was widow of

long, was under his sole jurisdiction, and much trouble
was caused the Consul by the lawless conduct of the rum-
corrupted natives. The traders were nick-named Palm-
oil Lambs,' and they used to call Burton their Shepherd,
and I believe he managed them very amicably. Never-
theless, in spite of pressure of business, and of the
dangerous character of the climate, our enthusiastic
traveller, supported by the better class of European agents
and super-cargos, still pursued his explorations with
ardour. He visited the coast from Bathust (Gambia) to
St. Paul de Loanda (Angola). He marched up to
Abeokuta, in December 1861. He ascended the Cameroon
Mountains, the wonderful extinct volcano described by
Hanno, the Carthaginian, and represented as the " Theon
Ochema " by Ptolemy. He advised the English Government to establish there a sanatarium for the West Coast,
and a convict station for garrotters, where they might

the King's uncle, the Regent, John Duke of Bedford, third son of
Henry IV.

Elizabeth Wydeville, above-mentioned, was grandmother of Lady
Eleanor Arundell, of Lankerne, and married secondly, King Edward
IV., by whom she was mother of the Prince of Wales, and Richard
Duke of York, who were supposed to have been murdered in the
Tower by command of Richard III.; Edward IV.'s daughters by
Elizabeth Wydeville were married—Anne to Thomas Howard, Duke
of Norfolk, and Elizabeth became the wife of Henry VII., and their
brother, the above-named Marquis of Dorset was Lady Arundell's
father, and therefore Queen Elizabeth was her granddaughter, and
was second cousin to Sir Thomas Arundell, the First Lord Arundell
of Wardour.

There is also a Royal descent from King Edward I. through his
son Thomas of Brotherton, Earl of Norfolk, and first Earl Marshal
of England, by the above-named marriage of Sir Thomas Arundell
with his cousin Lady Margaret Howard, whose sister, Lady Katharine
was the ill-fated wife of Henry VIII.; and their brother, Thomas
Howard, Duke of Norfolk, married another daughter of Edward IV.
who was aunt to Lady Arundell; (this descent gives the Arundells
the right to quarter the Plantagenet arms.)

C

be made useful in constructing roads and cultivating cotton and chocolate.

He offered Earl Russell, in those days, to supply one million pounds sterling per annum if made Governor of the Gold Coast, but Lord Russell answered him "that gold was becoming too common." In 1863 were published the result of Captain Burton's labours on the West African Coast in a work entitled, "Abeokuta and the Cameroon Mountains." After visiting, in April 1863, the cannibal Mpangwe (the Fans of Du Chaillu), whose accuracy he had suggested, and was now able to confirm, he proceeded to Benin City, unknown to the European world since the death of Belzoni. He vainly dug under the tree where the great Italian had been buried ; and thus could not carry out his ardént wish of bringing home Belzoni's bones to his native land.

His description of the surrounding region appeared in " Fraser's Magazine," for Feburary, March, and April, 1863, under the title of " Wanderings in West Africa ; " another "Wanderings in West Africa," in 2 vols., appeared shortly after. He next ascended the Elephant Mountain, an account of which was read before the Geographical Society, April 27th, 1863.

After a brief visit to England, for the re-establishment of his health, and a trip to Maderia and Tenerife, Captain Burton visited the line of lagoons between Lagos and the Volta River, explored the Yellalah Rapids of the Congo River, and spent a few days with the King Dàhome. Invited by this potentate to pass the three winter months with him, and directed by the Foreign Office, he returned to Aghome, the capital, as British Commissioner, with presents from Her Majesty, and witnessed the celebrated annual " customs," which he was sent to induce the King to abolish. The sights he was daily

compelled to see would have injured most men's nerves
for life. Earl Russell said he performed this delicate
and dangerous mission to his perfect satisfaction. This
is described in " A mission to Gelele, King of Dáhome."*
Captain Burton's other works upon West Africa are an
"Essay on the Nile Basin,"† and a Collection of 2,859
Proverbs, being an attempt to make the Africans delineate
themselves.‡ At this juncture (1865) our traveller came
to London, between his African and Brazilian career;
and a public dinner was given in his honour, at which
Lord Derby (then Lord Stanley) took the chair, and
made a speech which deserves to be recorded. (See
Appendix B.)

Having spent ten years, on and off, in Africa, Captain
Burton was transferred by the Foreign Office to the
Consulship of Santos, São Paulo, in Brazil. Here he
passed four years, and was equally active and useful,
both on the coast and the interior. He thoroughly ex-
plored his own province, which is larger than France;
the Gold mines and Diamond diggings of Minas
Geraes, and he canoed down the great river São
Francisco, 1500 miles. This adventure is described in
" The Highlands of the Brazil."§ He also visited the
Argentine Republic, and the rivers Plata-Paraná and
Paraguay, for the purpose of reporting the state of the
Paraguayan War to the Foreign Office. He crossed the
Pampas and the Andes to Chili and Peru, amongst the
" bad Indians," whilst on sick leave for an illness during
which he was at death's door; and he visited the Pacific
Coast, to inspect the scenes of the earthquake at Arica,
returning by the Straits of Magellan, Buenos Ayres, and
Rio de Janeiro, to London.‖ After six weeks' rest our

* 2 vols., Tinsleys, 1864.　　　　† Tinsleys, 1864.
‡ Tinsleys, 1865.　　　　§ 2 vols., Tinsleys, 1869.
‖ " Letters from the Battle-field of Paraguay." Tinsleys, 1871.

explorer was appointed to Damascus, where his friendship with Mahometans and his knowledge of Arabic and
Persian (the language of literature) put him in intimate
relation with the Arab tribes and all the chief authorities.
He is the only man, not born a Moslem and an Oriental,
who has performed the Hajj to Meccah and Medinah,
and yet can live with the Moslems in perfect friendship.
The " True Believers," in fact, consider him a *Persona
grata*, something more civilized than the common run of
Franks. They call him Haji Abdullah, and treat him as
one of themselves.

In 1869, Lord Derby (then Lord Stanley), whose
sound sense and great judgment knew exactly the man
to suit the post, and the post the man, approved of the
appointment, which had excited not a little jealousy.
Captain Burton raised the English name to its old pres-
tige. Besides exploring all the unknown parts of Syria,
Palestine, and the Holy Land, he saved the poor pea-
santry of Damascus from the usurers ; he advanced the
just claims of British subjects ; he kept the peace when
a massacre appeared imminent, and he opposed the fana-
tical persecution against the Christians. He was just
the man to be in the way of a corrupt Turkish Governor-
General—Rashid Pasha—who applied officially for his
recall. Lord Derby's successor in office, ever com-
plaisant and polite to foreigners, acceded to this ab-
normal proceeding without inquiry, and from this date
began the ruin of Damascus, and the visible and speedy
decline of Syria.

Captain Burton, thrown out of employment for ten
months, proceeded to Iceland, explored, and thoroughly
studied it.* During his absence Lord Granville, having
found out the truth, and the relative positions and con-

* " Ultima Thule," &c. 2 vols., Nimmo, 1875.

duct of Rashid Pasha and Captain Burton, compensated
the latter by the Consulate of Trieste. There the explorer has made himself familiar with every spot of
ground within a hundred miles, and learnt the languages
and politics of that lively corner of the world. He has
explained and described all the surrounding *castellieri*, or
pre-historical buildings of Istria—previously supposed
to be Roman—unknown to the literary world. They
are considered to be the most interesting in the continent of Europe.

Captain Burton, having six months' leave, went to
India in December, 1875, to revisit, and to show his wife,
his old quarters and travels during his many years'
active service in India, which commenced his career
under Sir Charles Napier. On his return he brought
out a work called "Sind Revisited."*

In the autumn of 1876 notices came of the distress of
Egypt. In his old Arab days, twenty-five years ago,
wandering about with his Korán, he ascertained the
existence of a gold land in that part of Arabia belonging
to Egypt. He was then, his wife tells us, a "romantic
youth, with a chivalrous contempt for filthy lucre, and
only thought of winning his spurs." So he turned away
and passed on. After a quarter of a century, seeing
Egypt in absolute distress, he asked for "leave;" he
went to Cairo and imparted his secret to the Khedive,
who equipped an expedition in a few days and sent him
there (1876) to rediscover the land. That expedition is
recounted in the "Gold Mines of Midian."† The Khedive was desirous of despatching him a second time, with
a view to learning exactly every detail of this rich old
country, and he set out again for Cairo in October, 1877,
and in December was in command of a new expedition

* 2 vols., Bentley, 1877.   † C. Kegan Paul, 1878.

on a much larger scale, leaving his wife with orders to bring the last-named book through the Press, and then join him. She finished her work in January, 1878 : then she proceeded to Suez, where she passed the winter, endeavouring in vain to find the expedition, which remained some five months in the desert of North-West Arabia doing hard work. He discovered, on the coast, a region of gold and silver, turquoise, agate, and pearls; of lead, and six or seven commoner metals extending some hundreds of miles either way; a Roman temple, and thirty-two old mining cities. The expedition mapped, planned, and sketched the whole country, and returned in triumph, bringing twenty-five tons of various minerals for analysis. The ancients had worked only forty feet deep, whereas with modern appliances 1000 or 1200 would be feasible. On the arrival of the expedition at Suez in April, 1878, the Khedive sent a special train to bring back Captain Burton and his Staff to Cairo, and desired him to make an exhibition of his trophies, which His Highness opened in person. Captain Burton then returned to Trieste, where he remained to report on the the then expected war in Bosnia and Herzegovina. He was finally allowed to come to London in July, 1878, to subject the minerals to every possible assay; to report to Egypt, and to form and carry out some immediate plan of action in regard to the Land of Midian. Notwithstanding the variety of business to be transacted in London within a few months, Captain Burton found time to produce a work on his late expedition entitled " The Land of Midian Revisited,"* and a cheap edition of " Meccah and Medinah."† Mrs. Burton produced at the same time a work called " A.E.I. Arabia, Egypt, and

* 2 vols., C. Kegan Paul & Co., 1879.
† William Mullan & Son, 1879.

India,"* and a cheap edition of her first work, "Inner Life of Syria."† Captain Burton and his wife are now gone forth again, to pass the hot months at his post at Trieste, and the cold months in working the mines of Midian, in Arabia, which may occupy them some two or three years. Of their life in Trieste, a passer by on the Staff of the lively *World* paid them a visit, and wrote the following "Celebrity at Home," which appeared in the issue of the 27th November, 1878. As it illustrates their lives and characters so well, besides giving a very fair idea of Trieste, I think it worth while to insert it here.

* William Mullan & Son, 1879.
† 2 vols., C. Kegan Paul & Co., 1875.

"CELEBRITY AT HOME."

Captain Richard F. Burton at Trieste.

It is not given to every man to go to Trieste. The fac
need not cause universal regret, inasmuch as the chief
Austrian port on the Adriatic, shares with Oriental towns
the disagreeable character of presenting a fair appearance from a distance, and afflicting the traveller, who
has become for the time a denizen, with a painful sense
of disenchantment. Perhaps the first glimpse of Trieste
owes something to contrast, as it is obtained after passing through a desolate stony wilderness called the Karso.
As the train glides from these inhospitable heights towards Trieste, the head of the Adriatic presents a scene
of unrivalled beauty. On one side rise high, rugged,
wooded mountains, on a ledge of which the rails are laid;
on the other is a deep precipice, at whose base rolls the
blue sea, dotted with lateen sails, painted of every shade
of colour, and adorned with figures of saints and other
popular devices. The white town staring out of the
corner covers a considerable space, and places its villa
outposts high up the neighbouring hills, covered with
verdure to the water's edge.

Trieste is a polyglot settlement of Austrians,
Italians, Slavs, Jews, and Greeks, of whom the two
latter monopolise the commerce. It is a City dear and
unhealthy to live in, over-ventilated and ill-drained.
t might advantageously be called the City of three

winds. One of these, the *Bora*, blows the people almost
into the sea with its fury, rising suddenly, like a
cyclone, and sweeping all before it; the second is
named the *Scirocco*, which blows the drainage back into
the town; and the third is the *Contraste*, formed by the
two first-named winds blowing at once against each
other. Alternating atmospherically between extremes
of heat and cold, Trieste is, from a political point of
view, perpetually pushing the principles of independence
to the verge of disorder.

Arrived at the railway station, there is no need to call
a cab and ask to be driven to the British Consul's, since,
just opposite the station and close to the sea, rises the
tall block of building in which the Consulate is situated.
Somewhat puzzled to choose between three entrances,
the stranger proceeds to mount the long series of steps
lying beyond the particular portal to which he is directed.
There is a superstition, prevalent in the building and in
the neighbourhood, that there are but four stories, including but one hundred and twenty steps. Whoso,
after a protracted climb, finally succeeds in reaching
Captain Burton's landing, will entertain considerable
doubts as to the correctness of the estimate. A German
damsel opens the door, and inquires whether the visitor
wants to see the Gräfin (Countess) or the Herr Consul.

Captain and Mrs. Burton are well, if airily lodged on
a flat composed of ten rooms, separated by a corridor
adorned with a picture of our Saviour, a statuette of
St. Joseph with a lamp, and a Madonna with another
lamp burning before it. Thus far, the belongings are
all of the Cross; but no sooner are we landed in the
little drawing-rooms than signs of the Crescent appear.
Small but artistically arranged, the rooms, opening into
one another, are bright with Oriental hangings, with

trays and dishes of gold and silver, brass trays and
goblets, chibouques with great amber mouthpieces, and
all kinds of Eastern treasures mingled with family
souvenirs. There is no carpet, but a Bedouin rug
occupies the middle of the floor, and vies in brilliancy of
colour with Persian enamels and bits of good old china.
There are no sofas, but plenty of divans covered with
Damascus stuffs. Thus far the interior is as Mussul-
man as the exterior is Christian : but a curious effect is
produced among the Oriental *mise en scène* by the presence
of a pianoforte and a compact little library of well-chosen
books. There is, too, another library here, greatly
treasured by Mrs. Burton, to wit, a collection of her
husband's works in about forty volumes. On the walls
are many interesting relics, models, and diplomas of
honour, one of which is especially prized by Captain
Burton. It is the *brevet de pointe* earned in France for
swordmanship. Near this hangs a picture of the Damascus home of the Burtons by Frederick Leighton.

As the guest is inspecting this bright bit of colour he
will be roused by the full strident tones of a voice skilled
in many languages, but never so full and hearty as when
bidding a friend welcome. The speaker, Richard Burton,
is a living proof that intense work, mental and physical,
sojourn in torrid and frozen climes, danger from dagger
and from pestilence, "age" a person of good sound con-
stitution far less than may be supposed. A Hertfordshire
man, a soldier and the son of a soldier, of mingled Scotch,
Irish, and French descent, his iron frame shows in its
twelfth lustre no sign of decay. *Arme blanche* and more
insidious fever have neither dimmed his eye nor wasted
his sinews.

Standing about five feet eleven, his broad deep chest
and square shoulders reduce his apparent height very

considerably, and the illusion is intensified by hands and feet of Oriental smallness. The Eastern, and indeed distinctly Arab, look of the man is made more pronounced by prominent cheek-bones (across one of which is the scar of a sabre-cut), by closely-cropped black hair just tinged with gray, and a pair of piercing black, gipsy-looking eyes. A short straight nose, a determined mouth partly hidden by a black moustache, and a deeply-bronzed complexion lit by livid pallor, complete the remarkable physiognomy so wonderfully rendered on canvas by Leighton only a couple of seasons ago. It is not to be wondered at, that this stern Arab face, and a tongue marvellously rich in Oriental idiom, and Mahometan lore, should have deceived the doctors learned in the Koran, among whom Richard Burton risked his life during that memorable pilgrimage to Meccah and Medinah, on which the slightest gesture or accent betraying the Frank would have unsheathed a hundred Kandjars.

This celebrated journey, the result of an adventurous spirit worthy of a descendant of Rob Roy Macgregor, has never been surpassed in audacity or in perfect execution, and would suffice to immortalise its hero if he had not in addition explored Harar and Somali Land, organized a body of irregular cavalry in the Crimea, pushed (accompanied by Speke) into Eastern Africa from Zanzibar, visited the Mormons, explored the Cameroon Mountains, visited the King of Dahomey, traversed the interior of Brazil, made a voyage to Iceland, and last, but not least, discovered and described the Land of Midian.

Leading the way from the drawing-rooms or divans he takes us through bedrooms and dressing-rooms, furnished in Spartan simplicity with little iron bedsteads covered with bearskins, and supplied with reading-tables and lamps, besides which repose the Bible, the Shakespeare, the Euclid, and the Breviary which go with Captain and Mrs. Burton on all their wanderings. His gifted wife, one of the Arundells of Wardour, is, as becomes a scion of an ancient Anglo-Saxon and Norman Catholic house, strongly attached to the Church of Rome; but religious opinion is never allowed to disturb the peace of the Burton household, the head of which is laughingly accused of Mahometanism by his friends. The little rooms are completely lined with rough deal shelves, containing perhaps a thousand or more volumes in every Western language, as well as in Arabic, Persian, and Hindostani. Every odd corner is piled with weapons, guns, pistols, boar-spears, swords of every shape and make, foils and masks, chronometers, barometers, and all kinds of scientific instruments. One cupboard is full of medicines necessary for Oriental expeditions or for Mrs. Burton's Trieste poor, and on it is written "The Pharmacy." Idols are not wanting, for elephant-nosed Gunpati is there cheek by jowl with Vishnu.

The most remarkable objects in the three rooms just alluded to are the rough deal tables, which occupy most of the floor space. They are almost like kitchen or ironing-tables. There may be eleven of them, each covered with writing-materials. At one of them sits Mrs. Burton in morning *négligé*, a gray *choga*—the long loose Indian dressing-gown of soft camel's hair—topped by a smoking-cap of the same material. She rises and greets her husband's old friend with the cheeriest voice in the world. "I see you are looking at our tables. Every one does. Dick likes a separate table for every book, and when he is tired of one he goes to another.

There are no tables of any size in Trieste, so I had these made as soon as I came. They are so nice, we may upset the ink-bottle as often as we like without anybody being put out of the way. These three little rooms are our 'den,' where we live, work, and receive our *intimes*, and we leave the doors open that we may consult over our work. Look at our view!" From the windows, looking landward, one may see an expanse of country extending for thirty or forty miles, the hills covered with foliage, through which peep trim villas, and beyond the hills higher mountains dotted with villages, a bit of the wild Karso peering from above. On the other side lies spread the Adriatic, with Miramar, poor Maximilian's home and hobby, lying on a rock projecting into the blue water, and on the opposite coast are the Carnian Alps capped with snow.

" Why we live so high up," explains Captain Burton, " is easily explained. To begin with, we are in good condition, and run up and down the stairs like squirrels. We live on the fourth story because there is no fifth. If I had a *campagna* and gardens and servants, horses and carriages, I should feel tied, weighted down, in fact. With a flat and two or three maidservants, one has only to lock the door and go. It feels like ' light marching order,' as if we were always ready for an expedition ; and it is a comfortable place to come back to. Look at our land-and-sea-scape : we have air, light, and tranquillity ; no dust, no noise, no street smells. Here my wife receives something like seventy very intimate friends every Friday, an exercise of hospitality to which I have no objection, save one, and that is met by the height we live at. There is in every town a lot of old women of both sexes, who sit for hours talking about the weather and the *cancans* of the place, and this contingent cannot face the stairs."

In spite of all this, and perhaps because of it—for the famous Oriental traveller, whose quarter of a hundred languages are hardly needed for the entry of cargoes at a third-rate seaport, seems to protest too much—one is impelled to ask what anybody can find to do at Trieste, an inquiry simply answered by a " Stay and see," with a slap on the shoulder to enforce the invitation. The *ménage Burton* is conducted on the early-rising principle. About four or five o'clock our hosts are astir, and already in their " den" drinking tea made over a spirit-lamp, and eating bread and fruit, reading and studying languages. By noon the morning's work is got over, including the consumption of a cup of soup, the ablution without which no true believer is happy, and the obligations of Frankish toilette. Then comes a stroll to the fencing-school, kept by an excellent broadswordsman, an old German trooper. For an hour Captain and Mrs. Burton fence in the school, if the weather be cold; if it is warm they make for the water, and often swim for a couple of hours. Then comes a spell of work at the Consulate. " I have my Consulate," the Chief explains, " in the heart of the town. I don't want my Jack-tar in my sanctum; and when he wants *me,* he has usually been on the spree and got into trouble." While the husband is engaged in his official duties, the wife is abroad promoting a Society for the Prevention of Cruelty to Animals, a necessary institution in Southern countries, where—on the purely gratuitous hypothesis that the so-called lower animals have no souls—the uttermost brutality is shown in the treatment of them. " You see," remarks our host, " that my wife and I are like an elder and younger brother living *en garçon.* We divide the work. I take all the hard and scientific part, and make her do all the rest. When we have worked all day, and

said all we have to say to each other, we want relaxation.
To that end we have formed a little ' mess,' with fifteen
friends at the *table d'hôte* of the Hôtel de la Ville, where
we get a good dinner and a pint of the country wine
made on the hill-side for a florin and a half. By this
plan we escape the bore of housekeeping, and are re-
lieved from the curse of domesticity, which we both hate.
At dinner we hear the news, if any, take our coffee,
cigarettes, and Kirsch outside the hotel, then go home-
wards to read ourselves to sleep ; and to-morrow *da
capo.*

To the remark that this existence, unless varied by
journeys to Midian and elsewhere, would be apt to
kindle desires for fresher woods and newer pastures,
Captain Burton replies, " The existence you deprecate is
varied by excursions. I know every stick and stone for
a hundred miles round, and all the pre-historic remains
of the country-side. Our Austrian Governor-General,
Baron Pino de Friedenthal, is a first-rate man, and often
gives us a cruise in the Government yacht. It is, as you
say, an odd place for me to be in ; but recollect, it is not
every place that would suit *me.*"

The man, who, with his wife, has made this *pièd à terre*
in Trieste, is a man unlike anybody else—a very extraordinary man, who has toiled every hour and minute for
thirty-eight years, distinguishing himself in every possible way. He has done more than any other six men in
Her Majesty's dominions, and is one of the best, noblest,
and truest that breathes.

While not on active service, or on sick leave, he has
been serving his country, humanity, science, and civili-
zation in other ways, by opening up lands hitherto unknown, and trying to do good wherever he went. He

was the pioneer for all other living African travellers. He first attempted to open up the sources of the Nile. He " opened the oyster for the rest to take the pearl"— his Lake Tanganyika is the head basin of the Nile.

He has made several great expeditions under the Royal Geographical Society and the Foreign Office, most of them at the risk of his life. His languages, knowledge, and experience upon every subject, or any single act of his life, of which he has concentrated so many into thirty-eight years, would have raised any other man to the top of the ladder of honour and fortune.

We may sum up his career by their principal heads.

Nineteen years in the Bombay army, the first ten in active service, principally in the Sindh Survey on Sir Charles Napier's Staff. In the Crimea, Chief of the Staff to General Beatson, and the chief organiser of the Irregular Cavalry.

Several remarkable and dangerous expeditions in unknown lands. He is the discoverer and opener of the Lake Regions of Central Africa, and perhaps the Senior Explorer of England.

He has been nineteen years in the Consular service in the four quarters of the Globe,—Africa, Asia, South America, and Europe—doing good service everywhere. It would be impossible to enumerate *all* that Captain Burton has done in the last forty years; but we cannot pass over his knowledge of twenty-nine languages, European and Oriental—not counting dialects—and now that Mezzofante is dead we may call him the Senior Linguist. Nor can we omit the fact that he has written about forty standard works, a list of which will appear at the end of this memoir. (See Appendix D.)

He is a man incapable of an untruth, or of truckling to what finds favour. His wife tells us in her " Inner

Life of Syria" that "humbug stands abashed before him," that he lives sixty years before his time, and that, "born of Low Church and bigoted parents, as soon as he could reason he began to cast off prejudice and follow a natural law. Grace aiding the reason of man—upright, honourable, manly and gentlemanly, but professing no direct form of belief, except in One Almighty Being, God—the belief that says, " I do that because it is *right*—not for hell nor heaven, nor for religion, but because it is right—a natural law of Divine Grace, which such men unconsciously ignore as Divine intelligence: yet such it is."

Perhaps this is the secret of our finding so distinguished a Soldier, Government-Envoy, Foreign Office Commissioner, author, linguist, benefactor to science, Explorer, discoverer, and organizer of benefits to his country and mankind at large, standing before the world on a pedestal as a plain unadorned hero, sitting by his distant fireside in a strange land, bearing England's neglect, and seeing men who have not done a tithe of his service, reaping the credit and reward of his deeds—perhaps of the very ideas and words that he has spoken and written. For years he has thought, studied, and written, and in all the four quarters of the globe has been a credit to his country. For years he has-braved hunger, thirst, heat, and cold, wild beasts, savage tribes; has fought and suffered, carrying his life in his hand for England's honour and credit, and his country's praise and approbation, and done it nobly and successfully. But like many of the greatest heroes that have ever lived, his country will deny him the meed of success whilst he lives, and erect marble statues and write odes to his memory when he can no longer see and hear them—when God, who knows all, will be his reward.

Burton's lamented college friend Alfred Bates Richards, wrote two leading Articles expressing his opinions in the following outspoken and manly words, and if I quote them here, it is not by way of advertising any claim Burton may have, or of intoning any grumble against any Government, for to the best of my belief the Burton's have taken up a new line of their own. I quote them merely to show the estimation in which I believe him to be held by the whole Press of England since every Article is more or less written in the same tone with scarcely a dissentient pen, and I have selected these as two of the best specimens :—

"The best men in this world, in point of those qualities which are of service to mankind, are seldom gifted with powers of self-assertion in regard to personal claims, rewards, and emoluments. Pioneers, originators, and inventors are frequently shunted and pushed aside by those who manage, by means of arts and subtleties, (utterly unknown to men of true genius and greatness of character) to reap benefits and honours to which they are not in the slightest degree entitled. Sometimes a reaction sets in and the truth is discovered, when it is too late. There is no country which neglects real merit so frequently and so absolutely as England—none which so liberally bestows its bounties upon second and third-rate men, and sometimes absolute pretenders. The most daring explorer cannot find his way up official backstairs ; the most heroic soldier cannot take a *salon* or a *bureau* by storm. There are lucky as well as persevering individuals who succeed in the most marvellous way in obtaining far more than their deserts. We have heard of a certain foreigner, now dead, who held a lucrative position for many years in this country, that he so

pestered and followed up the late Lord Brougham that
he at last obtained the post he sought by simple force of
boredom and annoyance. Some men think they ought
not to be put in the position of postulants; but that
recognition of their services should be spontaneous on
the part of the authorities. They are too proud to ask
for that which they consider it is patent they have so
eminently deserved that it is a violation of common
decency to withhold it; and so they 'eat their hearts'
in silence, and accept neglect with dignity, if not
indifference.

"We do not intend to apply these remarks strictly to
the occasion which has suggested them. If we did not
state this, we should possibly injure the cause which we
are anxious to maintain. We have watched the career
of an individual for some thirty-five years with interest
and admiration, and we frankly own that we now think
it time to express our opinion upon the neglect with
which the object of that interest and admiration has been
treated. We alone are responsible for the manner in
which we record our sentiments. Captain Richard
Burton, now Her Majesty's Consul at Trieste, is, in our
judgment, the foremost traveller of the age. We shall
not compare his services or exploits with those of any
of the distinguished men who have occupied a more
or less prominent position, and whose services have been
recognised by the nation. He has been upwards of
thirty years actively engaged in enterprises, many of them
of the most hazardous description. We pass over his
career in the Bombay Army for nearly twenty years,
during which time he acquired that wonderful knowledge
of Eastern languages, which is probably unequalled by any
living linguist. We shall not give even the catalogue of
his varied and interesting works, which have been of equal

service to philology and geography. His system of Bayonet Exercise, published in 1855, is, we may observe, *en passant*, the one now-in use in the British army. He suffered the fate of too many of his brother officers of the Indian army when it was reduced, on changing hands, and when he was left without pension or pay. He was emphatically the first great African pioneer of recent times. It is not our intention to speak disparagingly of the late Captain Speke—far from it; but it should be remembered that Speke was Burton's lieutenant, chosen by him to accompany him in his Nile researches, and that when Burton was stricken down by illness that threatened to prove fatal, Speke pushed on a little way ahead, and reaped nearly the whole credit of the discovery. Lake Tanganyika was Burton's discovery, and it was his original theory that it contained the sources of the Nile. Never was man more cruelly robbed by fate of his just reward. Could Speke have arrived where he did without even the requisite knowledge of languages, manners of the people, &c., save under Burton's guidance? Burton's pilgrimage to Mecca and Medinah was one of the most extraordinary on record. In the expedition to Somaliland, as well as that to the Lake regions of Central Africa, Speke was second in command. In the former both were severely wounded, and cut their way out or surrounding numbers of natives with singular dash and gallantry, one of the party—Lieutenant Stroyan—being killed. Nor should the wonderful expedition, undertaken alone, to the walled town of Harar, where no European had even been known to penetrate before, be forgotten. On this occasion Captain Burton actually added a grammar and vocabulary of a language to the stores of the philologists His journey and work on California and the Mormon country preceded that of Mr. Hepworth Dixon.

He explored the West Coast of Africa from Bathurst, on
the Gambia, to St. Paulo de Loanda in Angola, and the
Congo River, visiting the Fans. But his visit to Dahome
was still more important, as he exposed the customs of
that blood-stained kingdom, and gave information valuable to humanity as well as to civilisation and science.
This alone ought to have obtained for him some high
honorary distinction; but he got nothing beyond an
expression of satisfaction from the Government then in
power. During his four years' Consulship in Brazil his
work was simply Herculean. He navigated the River
St. Francisco 1,500 miles in a canoe, visited the gold
and diamond mines, crossed the Andes, and explored the
Pacific Coast, affording a vast fund of information, political, geographical, and scientific, to the Foreign Office.
Next we find him Consul at Damascus, where he did
good work in raising English influence and credit. Here
he narrowly escaped assassination, receiving a severe
wound. He explored Syria, Palestine, and the Holy
Land, protected the Christian population from a massacre, and was recalled by the effete Liberal Government
because he was too good a man, Damascus being reduced to a Vice-Consulate in accordance with their
policy of effacement. He is now shelved at Trieste, but
has still managed to embellish his stay there by some
valuable antiquarian discoveries.

If a Consulate is thought a sufficient reward for such
a man and such services, we have no more to say. If
he has been fairly treated in reference to his Nile explorations, we have no knowledge of the affair, which we
narrowly watched at the time, no discernment, and no
true sense of justice. When the war with Ashanti broke
out, we expressed our opinion that Captain Burton
should have been attached to the expedition. During

the Crimean war he showed his powers of organization under General Beatson, whose Chief of the Staff he was, in training 4,000 irregular cavalry, fit, when he left them, to do anything and go anywhere. In short, he has done enough for half a dozen men, and to merit half a dozen K.C.B.'s. We sincerely trust that the present Government will not fail, amidst other acts of justice and good works, to bestow some signal mark of Her Majesty's favour upon Captain Richard Burton, one of the most remarkable men of the age, who has displayed an intellectual power and a bodily endurance through a series of adventures, explorations, and daring feats of travel, which have never been surpassed in variety and interest by any one man, and whose further neglectful treatment, should it take place, will be a future source of indignant regret to the people of England."

The following Article appeared when Burton wrote his "Nile Basin." I quote that part of it which refers to Burton, and expunge that which does not regard my immediate subject:—

"About a quarter of a century ago Richard Burton, who had gained only a reputation for eccentricity at Oxford, left that University for India and entered the Bombay army. There he devoted his spare time to the acquisition of Oriental languages, science, and falconry, in company with the chiefs of Scinde, and, amongst other things, wrote works on the language, manners, and sports of that country. We cannot trace his career, but it is well known that he has become one of the greatest linguists of the age, gifted with the rare if not unique capacity of passing for a native in various Oriental countries. In addition to this he is a good classical scholar, an accomplished swordsman, and a crack shot. His 'Pilgrimage to Mecca and Medina' was an extraordinary record of successful daring and wonderful impersonation of Oriental character. As an Afghan, and under the name of Mirza Abdullah, he left Southampton on his mission, after undergoing circumcision in order to avoid detection, and during the voyage on board the P. and O. steamer was only known to be a European to the Captain and an attaché of the Turkish Embassy returning to Constantinople. His pilgrimage was successful, and he is the only European ever known to have performed it. Perhaps, however, the story of the most remarkable of his performances is contained in his 'First Footsteps in Eastern Africa,' telling how, alone and unaccompanied, during the latter stages, even by his attendants, he penetrated the hitherto almost fabulous walled city of Harar, hob-nobbed with its ferocious and exclusive Sultan, and bestowed on philologists a grammar of a new language. The description of his lying down to sleep the first night in that walled city of barbaric strangers, ignorant of the reception he might receive at the Sultan's levée in the morning, is well worth perusal. Then came the episode, which first gave the name of Speke to the world—the expedition in the country of the Somali, on the coast of the Red Sea, when the cords of the tent of Burton, Speke, Herne and the hapless Stroyan were cut by a band of 150 armed Somali during the night, after the desertion of their Eastern followers. The escape of Burton was characteristic of the man. Snatching up an Eastern sabre, the first weapon he could grasp, he cut his way by sheer swordsmanship through the crowd, escaping with a javelin thrust through both cheeks. Speke, after receiving seventeen wounds, was captured, and also subsequently escaped, and Stroyan was killed. At this time Burton had taken Speke under his especial patronage, and made him the lieutenant of his expeditions. Subsequently came the search after the Sources of the Nile, in which both Burton and Speke figured; next Burton's expedition to Utah; his consulship at Fernando Po, and the exploration of the Cameron Mountains; and, finally, his world-famed mission to the blood-stained Court of Dahomey. Such is Captain Richard Burton, and such his work, briefly and imperfectly described.

It is known, at least to the geographical world, that between Burton and his *quondam* lieutenant, Speke, a feud existed after the latter had proclaimed himself the discoverer of the Sources of the Nile. The outline of the story is this. On the exploring expedition under Burton's command he was seized with a violent and apparently fatal illness which compelled him to pause on the path of discovery at an advanced point. Speke went on, and, returning first to England, succeeded in getting the ear of the Geographical Society and the Foreign Office, and organised another expedition independently of Burton. On his return from this he proclaimed at once to the world that he had solved the great mystery, and the news was received with universal congratulation and belief. In the race for fame—if " *honor est à Nilo*" be deemed, as it must be, the common motto of our daring travellers—Burton, shaken to the backbone by fever, disgusted, desponding, and left behind, both in the spirit and the flesh, was, in racing parlance, " nowhere." He had the sense to retire from the contest during the first burst of excitement, and let judgment go by default. He went to visit the Mormons, and thence, by an ascending scale in respect to the objects of his search, to leave a card or two in the forest residences of the Gorillas. In the meantime Speke

became one of the lions of the day, and scarcely recognised the services of his able Chief and Pioneer.
To him the good fortune, the honour, the success—to
Burton, nothing. The very name and existence of the
latter were, as far as possible, ignored. Yet he had commenced all, organised all, arranged all. His Oriental
acquirements and experiences had paved the way to at
least within the last few stages of the "discovery." This
is a matter to be regretted. Much more to be regretted
was the sad and singular catastrophe of Captain Speke's
untimely death. On that very day a great passage, not
of arms, but of intellect and knowledge, was fixed to take
place. Burton had challenged Speke to a discussion
before a select tribunal. The subject was the Nile, its
sources, and Speke's claim to their discovery.

On the fatal afternoon of the 16th September, 1864,
when Speke perished, Burton had met him at 1.30 p.m. in
the rooms of Section E. of the Bath Association. Their
meeting was silent and ominous. Speke, who, as we are
informed, had been suffering for some time from nervousness and depression of spirits, probably arising from the
trials to his health in an Eastern climate, left the room to
go out shooting, and never returned alive! Much cause
had Richard Burton to lament that untimely end. His
lips were, to a great extent, immediately sealed.
Humanity, feeling, and decency—nay, imperious neces-
sity, demanded this. What he has written is argumen-
tative and moderate. He speaks of his deceased rival
with commendation for those good qualities which he
allows him to have possessed. Burton is as dignified in
his style as if he were a true Oriental. Unhappily,
Speke is now no more, but Burton has maintained
throughout a chivalrous tone towards his deceased
adversary.

APPENDIX A.

WITH regard to Louis XIV. there are one or two curious and interesting legends in the Burton family, well authenticated, but wanting one link, which would make Richard Burton great-great-great-grandson of Louis XIV. of France, by a morganatic marriage; and another which would entitle him to an English baronetcy, dating from 1622.

One of the documents in the family is entitled, "A Pedigree of the Young family, showing their descent from Louis XIV. of France," and which runs as follows:—

Louis XIV. of France took the beautiful Countess of Montmorency from her husband and shut him up in a fortress. After the death of (her husband) the Constable de Montmorency, Louis *married* the Countess. She had a son called Louis le Jeune, who married Lady Primrose, then a widow; another document says "brought over to Ireland by Lady Primrose," then a widow; but, disgusted with the licentiousness of his father's Court, he sent his infant son over to England with his wife, and shortly after died. This Lady Primrose's maiden name was Drelincourt, and the baby was named Drelincourt after his godfather and guardian, Dean Drelincourt (of Armagh), who was the father of Lady Primrose. He grew up, was educated at Armagh, and was known as Drelincourt Young. He married, and became the father of Hercules Drelincourt Young, and also of Miss (Sarah) Young, who married Dr. John. Campbell, LL.D., Vicar-General of Tuam (ob. 1772). Sarah Young's brother the above-mentioned Hercules Young, had a son George, a merchant in Dublin, who had some French deeds and various documents, which proved his right to property in France.

The above-named Dr. John Campbell, by his marriage with Miss Sarah Young (rightly Lejeune, for they had changed the name from French to English), had a daughter, Maria Margaretta Campbell, who was Richard Burton's grandmother. The same Dr. John Campbell was a member of the Argyll family, and a first cousin of the " three beautiful Gunnings," and was Richard Burton's great-grandfather.

These papers (for there are other documents) affect a host of families in Ireland—the Campbells, Nettervilles, Droughts, Graves, Burtons, Plunketts, Trimlestons, and many more.

In 1875 *Notes and Queries* was full of this question, and the various documents, but it has never been settled.

The genealogy, if proved, would run thus :—
Louis XIV.

Son, Louis le Jeune (known as Louis Drelincourt Young), by Countess Montmorency; married to Lady Primrose (see Earl of Rosebery), daughter of Drelincourt, Dean of Armagh.

Daughter, Sarah Young; married to Dr. John Campbell, LL.D., Vicar-General of Tuam, Galway.

Daughter, Maria Margaretta Campbell; married to the Rev. Edward Burton, Rector of Tuam, Galway.

Son, Lieutenant-Colonel Joseph Netterville Burton, 36th Regiment.

Son, Richard Burton, whose biography we are now relating.

There was a Lady Primrose buried in the Rosebery vaults, by her express will, with a little casket in her hands, containing some royal secret, which was to die with her; and many think that it contains the missing link.

The wife of Richard Burton received, in 1875, two very tantalizing anonymous letters, which she published in *Notes and Queries*, but which she has never been able to turn to account, through the writer declining to come forward, *even secretly*.

One ran thus :—

" MADAM,—There is an old baronetcy in the Burton family to which you belong, dating from the reign of Edward III.—I rather believe *now in abeyance*—which it was thought Admiral Ryder Burton would have taken up, and which after his death can be taken up by your branch of the family. All particulars you will find by searching the Herald's Office; but I am positive my information is correct.—From one who read your letter in *N. and Q.*"

She shortly after received and published the second anonymous letter : but, though she made several appeals to the writer in *Notes and Queries*, no answer was obtained, and Admiral Ryder Burton eventually died.

" MADAM,—I cannot help thinking that if you were to have the records of the Burton family searched carefully at Shap, in Westmoreland, you would be able to fill up the link wanting in your husband's descent, from 1712 to 1750, or thereabouts. As I am *quite positive* of a baronetcy *being in abeyance* in the Burton family, and that *an old one*, it would be worth your while getting all the information you can from Shap and Tuam. The Rev.

Edward Burton, Dean of Killala and Rector of Tuam, whose niece he married—viz., a Miss Ryder, of the Earl of Harrowby's family, by whom he had no children. His second wife, a Miss Judge, was a descendant of the Otways, of Castle Otway, and connected with many leading families in Ireland. Admiral James Ryder Burton could, if he *would*, supply you with information respecting the missing link in your husband's descent. I have always heard that *de Burton* was the proper family name, and I saw lately that a *de Burton* now lives in Lincolnshire.

Hoping, madam, that you will be able to establish your claim to the baronetcy,

"I remain, yours truly,

"A READER OF *N. and Q.*

"P.S.—I rather think also, and advise your ascertaining the *fact*, that the estate of Barker Hill, Shap, Westmoreland, by the law of *entail*, will devolve, at the death of Admiral Ryder Burton, on your husband, Captain Richard Burton."

From the Royal College of Heralds, however, the following information was forwarded to Mrs. Richard Burton:—

There *was* a baronetcy in the family of Burton. The first was Sir Thomas Burton, Knight, of Stokestone, Leicestershire; created July 22nd, 1622, a baronet, by King James I. Sir Charles was the last baronet. He appears to have been in great distress—a prisoner for debt, 1712. He is supposed to have died without issue, when the title became extinct—at least nobody has claimed it since. If your husband can prove his descent from a younger son of any of the baronets, he would have a right to the title. The few years must be filled

up between 1712 and the birth of your husband's grandfather, which was about 1750; and you must prove that
the Rev. Edward Burton, Rector of Tuam in Galway,
your husband's grandfather (who came from Shap, in
Westmoreland, with his brother, Bishop Burton, of
Tuam), was descended from any of the sons of any of
the baronets named."

APPENDIX B.

ON Tuesday, April 4th, 1865, there was celebrated an event in London of such importance to Anthropological Science as to deserve an especial record in these pages. On this day the Anthropological Society of London celebrated the election into their Society of five hundred Fellows, by giving a public dinner to Captain Richard F. Burton, their senior vice-president. What took place on this occasion should be made known as widely as possible, as we think it cannot fail to have a beneficial influence on the progress of anthropological science in this country.

The Right Honourable Lord Stanley, M.P., F.R.S., F.A.S.L., took the chair, and was supported on the right by Captain Burton, the Honourable, now Lord, Arthur Russell, M.P., J. A. Hardcastle, Esq., M.P., General Sir Trevor Phillips, W. S. W. Vaux, Esq., R. Bagshaw, Esq.; and on his left by Lord Houghton, the late Dr. James Hunt (the lamented President of the Anthropological Society), Viscount Milton, Sir G. Synge, Bart., and Mr. G. Buckley Matthew, H.M. Minister to Central America.

At the end of the four tables there presided Mr. J. Frederick Collingwood, V.P.A.S.L., Dr. Berthold

Seemann, V.P.A.S.L., Dr. R. S. Charnock, Treasurer A.S.L.; and Mr. George E. Roberts, Hon. Sec. A.S.L.* Apologies for not being able to attend were received from Viscount Palmerston, Earl of Clarendon, Lord

* The Company was so numerous that it would be impossible to give all the names, but some of them were noted down:—
Rev. Henry F. Rivers, Rev. Harry Tudor, Rev. Maurice P. Clifford, D.D., H. G. Atkinson, Esq., F.S.A., F.A.S.L., S. E. Collingwood, Esq., F.G.S., F.S.A.L., George North, Esq., F.A.S.L., L. O. Pike, Esq., M.A.. F.A.S L., J. Reddie, Esq., F.A.S.L., H. Brookes, Esq., F.A.S.L., E. Hart. Esq., F.R.C.S., F.A S.L., E. Bellamy, Esq., F.A.S.L., F. Braby, Esq. F.G.S., M. Paris, Esq., F.A.S.L., Dr. C. Carter Blake, F.G.S., F.A.S.L., J. Moore, Esq., F.A S.L., A. Swinburne, Esq., F.A.S L., E. Tinsley, Esq. F A S.L., Captain J. Hastie, F.A.S.L., C. Brett, Esq., F.A.S.L., N. Trübner, Esq., F.A.S.L., W. Pinkerton, Esq., F.S.A., F.A.S.L., H. W. Jackson, Esq., F.A.S.L., R. B. N. Walker, Esq., F.A.S.L., H. Hotze, Esq., F.A.S L., A. Hector, F.A.S.L., G. Dibley, Esq., F.A.S.L , A. Wilson, Esq., Captain O'Kelly, E. Charlesworth, Esq., F.G.S., H. W. Bates, Esq., Assist.-Sec., R.G-S., R. Arundell, Esq., F.A.S.L., H. Butler, Esq., F.A.S L., S. Courtauld, Esq., F.A.S.L., C. Harcourt, Esq , F.A S.L., Lieutenant Arundell. R.N., J. Meyer Harris, Esq., F.A.S.L., Dr. Dickson, W. Fothergill Cooke, Esq., F.A.S.L., J. Rae, Esq., F.A.S.L., G. F. Rankin, Esq., F A.S.L., W. Chamberlain, Esq., F.A.S. L., Wentworth Scott, Esq., F.A.S.L., Dr. J. F. Caplin, F.A.S.L., C. Stenning, Esq., F.A.S.L., E. Owen Tudor, Esq., E. Wilson, Esq. F.A.S.L., A. Spowers, Esq., N. J. Bagshawe, Esq., Dr. George Bird, R. H. W. Dunlop, Esq., C.B., H. Wood, Esq., A. Dick, Esq., A. C. Finlay, Esq., F.R.G.S., John Watson, Esq., Edward Dicey, Esq., H. K. Spark, Esq., G. F. Aston, Esq., W. H. Mitchell, Esq, M.A., F.A S L., Hon. E. T. O'Sullivan, F.A.S L., Colonel A. B. Richards, F.A.S.L., J. McDonald, Esq., Captain Rankin Hutchinson, F.A.S.L., Samuel Lucas, Esq., M.A., J. N. Lockyer, Esq , F.A.S.L., Mr. Ayres, &c.
The following gentlemen we understood had taken tickets, but were unable to attend :—
W. Stirling, Esq., M.P., Sir Andrew Smith, C.B., F.A.S.L., Sir George Denys, F.G.S. Dr. W. H. Russell, W. G. Smith, Esq., F.A.S.L., J. W. Conrad Cox, Esq., B.A , F.A.S.L., W. Travers, Esq., F.R.C.S., L.R.C.P., Colonel Showers, W. Salmon, Esq., F.G.S., Sutherland Edwards, Esq., Dr. J. Kirk, W. Wilson, Esq., C. Blake, Esq., J. M. Hepworth, Esq., F.A.S.L , J.P., H. Gooch, Esq., F.A.S.L.

Malmesbury, Viscount Strangford, who said that in his opinion Captain Burton was "the most distinguished traveller of modern times;" Lord Egerton, Lord Clifford, Sir Charles Wood, Bart., Mr. Whiteside, M.P., Sir R. Gerard, Bart. (now Lord Gerard de Bryn), Sir Charles Nicholson, Bart., Sir R. I. Murchison, K.C.B., Professor Owen, Mr. Henry Reeve, Major-General A. Scott Waugh, Colonel Stanley, Dr. Livingstone, Rev. Dunbar I. Heath, Mr. Laurence Oliphant, Dr. A. Barton, Rev. W. Monk, Mr. C. Robert des Ruffières, Major-General Hodgson, T. King Watts, Esq., F.A.S.L., Rev. Henry Clare, F.A.S.L.

After the Health of the Queen, The Prince and Princess of Wales, The Army and Navy and Volunteers,

The noble Chairman, in proposing "The Health of Captain Burton," said :—" I rise to propose a toast which will not require that I should bespeak for it a favourable consideration on your part. I intend to give you the health of the gentleman in whose honour we have met to-night. I propose the health of one—your cheers have said it before me—of the most distinguished explorers and geographers of the present day. I do not know what you feel, but as far as my limited experience in that way extends, for a man to sit and listen to his own eulogy is by no means an unmixed pleasure ; and in Captain Burton's presence I shall say a great deal less about what he has done than I should take the liberty of doing if he were not here. But no one can dispute this, that into a life of less than forty-five years Captain Burton has crowded more of study, more of hardship, and more of successful enterprise and adventure than would have sufficed to fill up the existence of half-a-dozen ordinary men. If, instead of continuing his active career—as we hope he will for many years to

come—it were to end to-morrow, he would still have
done enough to entitle him to a conspicuous and per-
manent place in the annals of geographical discoverers.
I need not remind you, except in the briefest way, of the
long course of his adventures and their results. His
first important work, the 'History of the Races of
Sindh' will long continue to be useful to those whose
studies lie in that direction, and those who, like myself,
have travelled through that Unhappy Valley—through
that young Egypt, which is about as like old Egypt as
a British barrack is like an Egyptian pyramid—will
recognize the fact that if there have been men who have
described that country for utilitarian purposes more
accurately and minutely, no man has described it with
a more graphic pen. With respect to his pilgrimage to
Meccah, that, I believe, was part only of a much larger
undertaking which local disturbances in the country prevented being carried out to the fullest extent. I do not
think I am exaggerating when I say that not more than
two or three Englishmen would have been able to per-
form that feat. The only two parallels to it that I
recollect in one generation are the exploring journeys of
Sir Henry Pottinger into Beloochistan, and the journey
of M. Vámbéry through the deserts of Central Asia. I
am speaking only by hearsay and report, but I take the
fact to be this, that the ways of Europeans and Asiatics
are so totally different—I do not mean in those important
acts to which we all pay a certain amount of attention
while we do them, but in those little trifling details of
everyday life that we do instinctively and without paying
attention to them—the difference in these respects between the two races is so wide that the Englishman who
would attempt to travel in the disguise of an Oriental
ought to be almost Oriental in his habits if he hope to

carry out that personation successfully. And if that be true of a journey of a few days, it is far more true of a journey extending over weeks and months, where you have to keep your secret, not merely from the casual observer, but from your own servants, your own friends, and your own travelling companions. To carry through an enterprise of that kind may well be a strain on the ingenuity of any man, and though, no doubt, danger does stimulate our faculties, still it does not take from the merit of a feat that it is performed under circumstances in which, in the event of detection, death is almost certain. I shall say nothing in this brief review of that plucky though unsuccessful expedition to the Somali country, which so nearly deprived the Anthropological Society of one of its ablest members. But I cannot pass over so lightly the journey into Harar—the first attempt to penetrate Eastern Africa in that quarter. That journey really opened a wide district of country previously unknown to the attention of civilized man. It led the way indirectly to the Nile expeditions, which lasted from 1856 to 1859. With respect to the labours which were gone through in those expeditions, and the controversies which arose out of those labours, I do not require here to say anything, except to make one passing remark. With regard to this disputed subject of the Nile, I may be permitted to say—though those who are experienced in geographical matters may treat me as a heretic—I cannot help it if they do, for I speak only by the light of common sense; but it seems to me that there is a little delusion in this notion of searching for what we call the source of a river. Can you say of any river that it has a source? It has a mouth, that is certain; but it has a great many sources, and, to my mind you might just as well talk of a plant as having only one root, or a man only one hair on his head, as of a river having a single source. Every river is fed from many sources, and it does not seem to me that the mere accident of hitting upon that which subsequent investigation may prove to be the largest of its many affluents is a matter about which there need be much controversy. The real test of the value of this kind of work is, what is the quantity of land previously unknown which the Discoverer has gone through, and which he has opened up to the knowledge of civilized man? Judged by that test, I do not hesitate to say that the African expedition of 1856 has been the most important of our time; the only rival which I could assign to it being that separate expedition which was undertaken by Dr. Livingstone through the southern part of the Continent. Where one man has made his way many will follow, and I do not think it is too sanguine an anticipation, negro Chiefs and African fevers notwithstanding, to expect that within the lifetime of the present generation we may know as much of Africa,—at least of Africa north of the equator and within fifteen degrees south of it,—as we know now of South America. Well, gentlemen, no man returns from a long African travel with health entirely unimpaired, and our friend was no exception to the rule. But there are men to whom all effort is unpleasant, so there are men to whom all rest, all doing nothing, is about the hardest work to which they could be put, and Captain Burton recruited his health, as you all know, by a journey to the Mormon country, travelling 3000 miles by sea and land, and bringing back from that community—morally, I think, the most eccentric phenomenon of our days—a very curious and interesting, and, as far as I could judge, the most accurate description we have yet received. Now, as to the last phase of the career which I am attempting to sketch—the embassy to Dahome, the discovery of the Cameroon Mountains, and the travels along the African coast, I shall only remind you of it, because I am quite sure that the published accounts must be fresh in all your minds. I do not know what other people may think of these volumes, but to me they were a kind of revelation of Negro life and character, enabling me to feel, which certainly I never felt before, that I could understand an African and barbarian Court. As to any theories arising out of these journeys, as to any speculations which may be deduced from them, I do not comment upon these here. This is not the place nor the occasion to do it. All I will say about them is, that when a man with infinite labour, with infinite research, and at the imminent risk of his life, has gone to work to collect a series of facts, I think the least the public can do is to allow him a fair hearing when he puts his own interpretation upon those facts. I will add this, that in matters which we all feel to be intensely interesting, and upon which we all know that our knowledge is imperfect, any man does us a service who helps us to arrange the facts which we have at our command ; who stimulates inquiry and thought by teaching us to doubt instead of dogmatising. I am quite aware that this is not in all places a popular theory. There are a great many people who, if you give them a new idea, receive it almost as if you had offered them personal violence. It puts them out. They don't understand it—they are not used to it. I think that state of the public mind, which we must all acknowledge, is the very best defence for the existence of Scientific Societies such as that to which so many of us belong. It is something for a man who has got a word to say to know that there is a Society where he will get a fair and considerate hearing; and, whether the judgment goes against him or not, at least he will be met by argument and not by abuse.

I think Captain Burton has done good service to the State in various ways. He has extended our knowledge of the globe on which we live ; and, as we happen to be men, and not mere animals, that is a result which, though it may not have any immediate utilitarian result, we ought to value. He has done his share in opening savage and barbarous countries to the enterprise of civilized man, and though I am not quite so sanguine as many good men have been as to the reclaiming of savage races, one has only to read his and all other travellers' accounts of African life in its primitive condition, to see that whetherthey gain much or not by European intercourse, at any rate they have nothing to lose.

But there is something more than that. In these days of peace and material prosperity (and both of them are exceedingly good things), there is another point of view in which such a career as that of our friend is singularly useful.

It does as much as a successful campaign to keep up in the minds of the English people that spirit of adventure and of enterprize, that looking to reputation rather than to money, to love of effort rather than to ease,— the old native English feeling which has made this country what it has become, and which, we trust, will keep this country what it is to be,—a feeling which, no doubt, the tendency of great wealth and material prosperity is to diminish ; but a feeling which, if it were to disappear from among us, our wealth and our material prosperity would not be worth one year's purchase.

Gentlemen, I propose the health of Captain Burton, and my best wish for him is that he may do for himself what nobody else is likely to do for him, that by his future perrormance he may efface the memory of his earlier exploits.

The toast was then drunk with three times three.

Captain Burton, who, on rising, was greeted with loud and protracted cheering, said :—

My Lord Stanley, my Lords and Gentlemen,—It falls to the lot of few men to experience a moment so full of gratified feeling as this, when I rise to return thanks for the honour you have done me on this, to me, most memorable occasion. I am proud to see my poor labours in the cause of discovery thus publicly recognized by the representative of England's future greatness. The terms of praise which have fallen from your lordship's lips are far above my present deserts, yet I treasure them gratefully in my memory as coming from one so highly honoured, not only as a nobleman, but as a man. I am joyed when looking round me to see so many faces of friends who have met to give me God-speed—to see around me so many of England's first men, England's brains, in fact ; men who have left their mark upon the age,—men whose memories the world will not willingly let die. These are the proudest laurels a man can win, and I shall wear them in my heart of hearts that I may win more of them on my return.

But, however gratifying this theme, I must bear in mind the occasion which thus agreeably brings us together. We meet to commemorate the fact that on March 14th, 1865, that uncommonly lusty youth, our young Anthropological Society, attained the respectable dimensions of five hundred members. My lord and gentlemen, it is with no small pride that I recall to mind how, under the auspices of my distinguished and energetic friend Dr. James Hunt, our present president,—and long

may he remain so,—I took the chair on the occasion of
its nativity. The date was January 6th, 1863. The
number of those who met was eleven. Each had his own
doubts and hopes, and fears touching the viability of the
new-born. Still we knew that our cause was good; we
persevered, we succeeded.

The fact is, we all felt the weight of the great want.
As a traveller and a writer of travels during the last
fifteen years, I have found it impossible to publish those
physiological observations, always interesting to our
common humanity, and at times so valuable. The
Memoirs of the Anthropological Society acts good Samaritan
to facts which the publisher and the drawing-room table
proudly pass by. Secondly, there was no arena for the
public discussion of opinions now deemed paradoxical,
and known to be unpopular. The rooms of the
Anthropological Society now offer a refuge to destitute
truth. There any man, monogenist or polygenist,
eugenestic, or dysgenestic, may state the truth as far as
is in him. No. 4, St. Martin's Place, we may truly call
the room

> " Where, girt by friend or foe,
> A man may say the thing he will."

All may always claim equally from us a ready hearing,
and what, as Englishmen, we prize the most, a fair field
and plenty of daylight.

And how well we succeeded—how well our wants
have been supplied by the officers of our society, we
may judge by this fact :—During the last twenty days
not less than thirty members have, I am informed by my
friend Dr. C. Carter Blake, been added to the five
hundred of last month. I confidently look forward to
the day when, on returning from South America, I shall
find a list of 1,500 names of our Society. We may say

vires acquirit eundo, which you will allow me to translate, "We gain strength by our go," in other words, our progress. This will give us weight to impress our profession and opinions upon the public. Already the learned of foreign nations have forgotten to pity us for inability to work off the grooves of tradition and habit. And we *must* succeed so long as we adhere to our principles of fair play and a hearing to every man.

I would now request your hearing for a few words of personal explanation, before leaving you for some years. I might confide it to each man separately, but I prefer the greatest possible publicity. It has come to my ears that some have charged me with want of generosity in publishing a book which seems to reflect upon the memory of Captain Speke. Without entering into details concerning a long and melancholy misunderstanding, I would here briefly state that my object has ever been, especially on this occasion, to distinguish between personal and scientific differences. I did not consider myself bound to bury my opinions in Speke's grave; to me, living, they are of importance. I adhere to all I have stated respecting the Nile sources; but I must change the form of their expression My own statement may, I believe, be considered to be moderate enough. In a hasty moment, I appended one more, which might have been omitted—as it shall from all future editions. I may conclude this painful controversial subject, by stating that Mr. Arthur Kinglake, of Weston-Super-Mare, writes to me that a memorial bust of my lamented companion is to be placed this year in the shire-hall, Taunton, with other Somersetshire heroes, Blake and Locke. I have seen the bust in the studio of Mr. Papworth, and it is perfect. If you all approve, it would give me the greatest pleasure to propose a subscription for the purpose before we leave this room.

And now I have already trespassed long enough upon your patience. I will not excuse myself, because I am so soon to leave you. Nor will I say adieu, because I shall follow in mind all your careers; yours, my Lord Stanley, to that pinnacle of greatness for which Nature and Fortune have destined you; and yours, gentlemen and friends, each of you, to the high and noble missions to which you are called. Accompanied by your good wishes, I go forth on mine with fresh hope, and with a vigour derived from the wholesome stimulus which you have administered to me this evening. My Lord Stanley, my Lords and Gentlemen, I thank you from my heart.

Lord Houghton then proposed the Diplomatic and Consular services. Lord Stanley, Success to the Anthropological Society. Dr. Hunt, the energetic President, made a very charming speech. The late Viscount Milton, Mr. R. B. N. Walker, Mr. Hardcastle, M.P., General Sir Trevor Phillips, Mr. Fred Collingwood, Lieutenant Arundell, R.N., The Honourable Arthur Russell, M.P., Captain Hastie, Dr. Seemon, Mr. Reddie, Mr. Algernon Swinburne, Mr. Lockyer, Mr. Samuel Lucas, Mr. Charlesworth, Mr. Mathew, Mr. Nicholas Trubner, Dr. C. Carter Blake, Mr. Roberts, Dr. Richard Charnock, made each speeches relative to the Society, to Captain Burton, or proposed and returned thanks for the several toasts.

At the end of the evening Dr. Hunt, the President, paid the compliment to Captain Burton of proposing the health of his wife; to which Captain Burton, in his usual grave, jocose way, made a reply, which caused much laughter—Mrs. Burton being in the gallery, behind a screen, all the while.

Dr. Hunt, President of the Anthropological Society, said : " He should be very sorry if they were to separate on that occasion, when they had met to bid farewell to Captain Burton, without drinking the health of one on whom they all looked with respect and admiration— Mrs. Burton. He felt it, therefore, to be their duty to join most heartily in drinking long health and prosperity to Mrs. Burton, and may she be long spared to take care of her husband when far away in South America. Those who paid homage to her paid homage also to him whom they had met to honour, and the more they knew of him the more they respected him."

Captain Burton : " I only hope, in the name of heaven, that Mrs. Burton won't hear of this."

Dr. Hunt said that, "as Captain Burton refused to respond to the toast in a proper manner, he must return thanks for Mrs. Burton. She begged him to say that she had great difficulty in keeping her husband in order, but that she would do what she could to take care of him, and to make him as innocent a man as they believed him to be."

APPENDIX C.

There are likewise some interesting events, connected with the last hours of the Great Napoleon and the Burtons, in the person of Francis Burton, Esq., of the 66th Regiment, Richard Burton's uncle, very agreeably told by Mrs. Ward, whose husband, then an Ensign, now a General, played a conspicuous part.

FACTS CONNECTED WITH THE LAST HOURS OF NAPOLEON.

BY MRS. WARD.

On the night of the 5th of May, 1821, a young ensign of the 66th Regiment, quartered at St. Helena, was wending his solitary way along the path leading from the plain of Deadwood to his barracks, situated on a patch of table-land called Francis Plain. The road was dreary, for to the left yawned a vast chasm, the remains of a crater, and known to the islanders as the " Devil's Punchbowl;" although the weather had been perfectly calm, puffs of wind occasionally issued from the neighbouring valleys; and, at last, one of these puffs having got into a gulley, had so much ado to get out of it, that it shrieked, and moaned, and gibbered, till it burst its bonds with a roar like thunder—and dragging up in its wrath, on its passage to the sea, a few shrubs, and one of those fair willows beneath which Napoleon,

first Emperor of France, had passed many a peaceful, if
not a happy, hour of repose, surrounded by his faithful
friends in exile.

This occurrence, not uncommon at St. Helena, has
given rise to an idea, adopted even by Sir Walter
Scott, that the soul of Napoleon had passed to another
destiny on the wings of the Storm Spirit; but, so far
from there being any tumult among the elements on that
eventful night, the gust of wind I have alluded to was
only heard by the few whose cottages dotted the green
slopes of the neighbouring mountains. But as that fair
tree dropped, a whisper fell among the islanders that
Napoleon was dead! No need to dwell upon what abler
pens than mine have recorded; the eagle's wings were
folded, the dauntless eyes were closed, the last words,
"*Tête d'armée*," had passed the faded lips, the proud
heart had ceased to beat. . . . !!

They arrayed the illustrious corpse in the attire iden-
tified with Napoleon even at the present day; and among
the jewelled honours of earth, so profusely scattered upon
the breast, rested the symbol of the faith he had pro-
fessed. They shaded the magnificent brow with the
unsightly cocked hat,* and stretched down the beautiful
hands in ungraceful fashion; every one, in fact, is familiar with the attitude I describe, as well as with a death-
like cast of the imperial head, from which a fine engraving
has been taken. The cast is true enough to nature, but
the character of the engraving is spoiled by the addition
of a laurel wreath on the lofty but insensate brow.

About this cast there is a *historiette* with which it is
time the public should become more intimately acquainted; it was the subject of litigation, the particulars

---

* The coffin being too short to admit this array in the order proposed, the hat was placed at the feet before interment.

of which are detailed in the *Times* newspaper of the 7th September, 1821, but to which I have now no opportunity of referring. Evidence, however, was unfortunately wanting at the necessary moment, and the complainant's case fell to the ground. The facts are these :—

The day after Napoleon's decease, the young officer I have alluded to, instigated by emotions which drew vast numbers to Longwood House, found himself within the very death-chamber of Napoleon. After the first thrill of awe had subsided, he sat down, and on the fly-leaf torn from a book, and given him by General Bertrand, he took a rapid but faithful sketch of the deceased Emperor. Earlier in the day, the officer had accompanied his friend, Mr. Burton, through certain paths in the island, in order to collect material for making a composition resembling plaster of Paris, for the purpose of taking the cast with as little delay after death as possible. Mr. Burton having prepared the composition, set to work and completed the task satisfactorily. The cast being moist, was not easy to remove; and, at Mr. Burton's request, a tray was brought from Madame Bertrand's apartments, Madame herself holding it to receive the precious deposit. Mr. Ward, the ensign alluded to, impressed with the value of such a memento, offered to take charge of at his quarters till it was dry enough to be removed to Mr. Burton's; Madame Bertrand, however, pleaded so hard to have the care of it that the two gentlemen, both Irishmen and soldiers, yielded to her entreaties, and she withdrew with the treasure, which she *never afterwards would resign.*

There can scarcely, therefore, be a question that the casts and engravings of Napoleon, now sold as emanating from the skill and reverence of Antommarchi, are from the original taken by Mr. Burton. We can only rest on circumstantial evidence, which the reader will allow is most conclusive. It is to be regretted that Mr. Burton's cast and that *supposed* to have been taken by Antommarchi were not *both* demanded in evidence at the trial in 1821.

The engraving I have spoken of has been Italianised by Antommarchi, the name inscribed beneath being *Napoleone.*

So completely was the daily history of Napoleon's life at St. Helena a sealed record, that on the arrival of papers from England, the first question asked by the islanders and the officers of the garrison was, "What news of Buonaparte ?" Under such circumstances, it was natural that an intense curiosity should be felt concerning every movement of the mysterious and ill-starred exile. Our young soldier one night fairly risked his commission for the chance of a glimpse behind the curtains of the Longwood windows; and, after all, saw nothing but the Imperial form, from the knees downwards. Every night, at sunset, a *cordon* of sentries was drawn round the Longwood plantations. Passing between the sentinels, the venturesome youth crept, under cover of trees, to a lighted window of the mansion. The curtains were not drawn, but the blind was lowered. Between the latter, however, and the window-frame, were two or three inches of space; so down knelt Mr. Ward! Some one was walking up and down the apartment, which was brilliantly illuminated.* The footsteps drew nearer, and Mr. Ward saw the diamond buckles of a pair of thin shoes; then two well-formed lower

* Napoleon's dining-room lamp, from Longwood, is, I believe, still in the possession of the 91st Regiment, it having been purchased by the officers at St. Helena in 1836.

limbs, encased in silk stockings; and, lastly, the edge of
a coat, lined with white silk. On a sofa, at a little distance, was seated Madame Bertrand, with her boy lean-
ing on her knee; and some one was probably writing
under Napoleon's dictation, for the Emperor was speaking
slowly and distinctly. Mr. Ward returned to his guard-
house, satisfied with having *heard the voice of Napoleon
Buonaparte.*

Mr. Ward had an opportunity of seeing the great
captive at a distance on the very last occasion that
Buonaparte breathed the outer air. It was a bright
morning when the serjeant of the guard at Longwood-
gate informed our ensign that "General Buonaparte"
was in the garden on to which the guard-room looked.
Mr. Ward seized his spy-glass, and took a breathless
survey of Napoleon, who was standing in front of his
house with one of his Generals. Something on the ground
attracted his notice ; he stooped to examine (probably a
colony of ants, whose movements he watched with interest), when the music of a band at a distance stirred
the air on Deadwood-plain, and he who had once led
multitudes forth at his slightest word, now wended his
melancholy way through the grounds of Longwood to
catch a distant glimpse of a British regiment under
inspection.

We have in our possession a small signal book, which
was used at St. Helena during the period of Napoleon's
exile. The following passages will give some idea of
the system of vigilance which it was thought necessary
to exercise, lest the world should again be suddenly
uproused by the appearance of the French Emperor on
the battle-field of Europe. It is not for me to offer any
opinion on such a system, but I take leave to say that I
never yet heard any British officer acknowledge that he

would have accepted the authority of Governor under the burden of the duties it entailed. In a word, although every one admits the difficulties and responsibilities of Sir Hudson Lowe's position, all deprecate the system to which he considered himself obliged to bend.

But the signal-book! Here are some of the passages which passed from hill to valley while Napoleon took his daily ride within the boundary prescribed:—

"General Buonaparte has left Longwood."
"General Buonaparte has passed the guards."
"General Buonaparte is at Hutt's-gate."
"General Buonaparte is missing."

The lattter paragraph resulted from General Buonaparte having, in the course of his ride, turned an angle of a hill, or descended some valley beyond the ken, for a few minutes, of the men working the telegraphs on the hills!

It was not permitted that the once Emperor of France should be designated by any other title than " *General* Buonaparte ;" and, alas! innumerable were the squabbles that arose between the Governor and his captive, because the British Ministry had made this puerile order peremptory. I have now no hesitation in making known the great Duke's opinion on this subject, which was transmitted to me two years ago, by one who for some months every year held daily intercourse with His Grace, but who could not, while the Duke was living, permit me to publish what had been expressed in private conversation.

"I would have taken care that he did not escape from St. Helena," said Wellington : "but he might have been addressed by any name he pleased."

I cannot close this paper without saying a word or two

on the condition of the buildings once occupied by the most illustrious and most unfortunate of exiles.

It is well known that Napoleon never would inhabit the house which was latterly erected at Longwood for his reception; that he said, "it would serve for his tomb;" and that the slabs from the kitchen *did* actually form part of the vault in which he was placed in his favourite valley beneath the willows, and near the fountain whose crystal waters had so often refreshed him.

This abode, therefore, is not invested with the same interest as his real residence, well named the "Old House at Longwood;" for a more crazy, wretched, filthy barn, it would scarcely be possible to meet with; and many painful emotions have filled my heart during nearly a four years' sojourn on "The Rock," as I have seen French soldiers and sailors march gravely and decorously to the spot, hallowed in their eyes, of course, by its associations with their invisible but unforgotten idol, and degraded, it must be admitted, by the change it has undergone.

Indeed, few French persons can be brought to believe that it ever was a decent abode; and no one can deny that it must outrage the feelings of a people like the French, so especially affected by associations, to see the bedchamber of their former Emperor a dirty stable, and the room in which he breathed his last sigh, appropriated to the purposes of winnowing and thrashing wheat! In the last-named room are two pathetic mementos of affection. When Napoleon's remains were exhumed in 1846, Counts Bertrand and Las Casas, carried off with them, the former a piece of the boarded floor on which the Emperor's bed had rested, the latter a stone from the wall pressed by the pillow of his dying Chief.

Would that I had the influence to recommend to the British Government, that these ruined, and I must add, desecrated, buildings should be razed to the ground; and that on their site should be erected a convalescent hospital for the sick of all ranks, of *both* services, and of *both* nations. Were the British and French Governments to unite in this plan, how grand a sight would it be to behold the two nations shaking hands, so to speak, over the grave of Napoleon!

On offering this suggestion, when in Paris lately, to one of the nephews of the first Emperor Napoleon, the Prince replied that "the idea was nobly philanthropic, but that England would never listen to it." I must add that his Highnes said this "rather in sorrow than in anger;" then, addressing Count L——, one of the faithful followers of Napoleon in exile, and asking him which mausoleum *he* preferred,—the one in which we then stood, the dome of the *Invalides*, or the rock of St. Helena,—he answered, to my surprise, "St. Helena; for no grander monument than that can ever be raised to the Emperor!"

Circumstances made one little incident connected with this, our visit to the *Invalides*, most deeply interesting. Comte D'Orsay was of the party; indeed it was in his elegant *atelier* we had all assembled, ere starting, to survey the mausoleum then being prepared for the ashes of Napoleon. Suffering and debilitated as Comte D'Orsay was, precious, as critiques on art, were the words that fell from his lips during our progress through the work-rooms, as we stopped before the sculptures intended to adorn the vault wherein the sarcophagus is to rest. Ere leaving the works, the Director, in exhibiting the solidity of the granite which was finally to encase Napoleon, struck fire with a mallet from the magnificent block:— "See," said Comte D'Orsay, "though the dome of the *Invalides* may fall, France may yet light a torch at the tomb of her Emperor." I cannot remember the exact words, but such was their import. Comte D'Orsay died a few weeks after this.

Since the foregoing was written, members of the Burton family have told me, that after taking the cast, Mr. Burton went to his regimental rounds, leaving the mask on the tray to dry; the back of the head was left on to await his return, not being dry enough to take off, and was thus overlooked by Madame Bertrand. When he returned he found that the mask was packed up and sent on board ship for France in Antommarchi's name. From a feeling of deep mortification he took the back part of the cast, reverently scraped off the hair now enclosed in a ring, and overcome by his feelings, dashed it into a thousand pieces. He was afterwards offered by Messrs. Gall and Spurzheim (phrenologists), one thousand pounds sterling for that portion of the cast which was wanting to the cast so-called Antommarchi's. Amongst family private papers there was a correspondence, read by most members of it, between Antommarchi and Mr. Burton, in which Antommarchi stated that he knew Burton had made the plaster and taken the cast. Mrs. Burton, after the death of her husband and Antommarchi, thought the correspondence useless and burnt it; but the hair was preserved under a glass watch-case in the family for forty years. There was an offer made about the year 1827 or 1828 by persons high in position in France who knew the truth to have the matter cleared up, but Mr. Burton was dying at the time, and was unable to take any part in it, so the affair dropped.

THE BUST OF BUONAPARTE.

Extract from the " NEW TIMES," *of September 7th*, 1821.

On Wednesday a case of a very singular nature occurred at the Bow Street Office.

Colonel Bertrand, the companion of Buonaparte in his exile at St. Helena (and the executor under his will), appeared before Richard Birnie, Esq., accompanied by Sir Robert Wilson, in consequence of a warrant having been issued to search the residence of the Count for a bust of his illustrious master, which, it was alleged, was the property of Mr. Burton, 66th Regiment, when at St. Helena.

The following are the circumstances of the case :—

Previous to the death of Buonaparte, he had given directions to his executors that his body should not be touched by any person after his death; however, Count Bertrand directed Dr. Antommarchi to take a bust of him; but not being able to find a material which he thought would answer the purpose, he mentioned the circumstance to Mr. Burton, who promised that he would procure some if possible.

The Englishman, in pursuance of this promise, took a boat and picked up raw materials on the island, some distance from Longwood. He made a plaster, which he conceived would answer this purpose. When he showed it to Dr. Antommarchi he said it would not answer, and refused to have anything to do with it, in consequence of which Mr. Burton proceeded to take a bust himself, with the sanction of Madame Bertrand, who was in the room at the time. An agreement was entered into that copies should be made of the bust, and that Messieurs Burton and Antommarchi were to have each a copy.

It was found, however, that the plaster was not

sufficiently durable for the purpose, and it was proposed to send the original to England to have copies taken.

When Mr. Burton, however, afterwards enquired for the bust, he was informed that it was packed and nailed up; but a promise was made, that upon its arrival in Europe, an application should be made to the family of Buonaparte for the copy required by Mr. Burton.

On its arrival Mr. Burton wrote to the Count to have his promised copy, but he was told, as before, that application would be made to the family of Buonaparte for it.

Mr. Burton upon this applied to Bow Street for a search warrant in order to obtain the bust, as he conceived he had a right to it, he having furnished the materials and executed it.

A warrant was issued, and Taunton and Salmon, two officers, went to the Count's residence in Leicester Square. When they arrived, and made known their errand, they were remonstrated with by Sir Robert Wilson and the Count, who begged they would not act till they had an interview with Mr. Birnie, as there must be some mistake. The officers politely acceded to the request, and waived their right of search.

Count Bertrand had, it seems, offered a pecuniary compensation to Mr. Burton for his trouble, but it was *indignantly refused by that officer*, who persisted in the assertion of his right to the bust as his own property, and made application for the search warrant.

Count Bertrand, in answer to the case stated by Mr. Burton, said that the bust was the property of the family of the deceased, to whom he was executor, and he thought he should not be authorised in giving it up. If, however, the law of this country ordained it otherwise, he must submit; but he should protest earnestly against it.

The worthy Magistrate, having sworn the Count to the fact that he was executor under the will of Buonaparte, observed that it was a case out of his jurisdiction altogether, and if Mr. Burton chose to persist in his claim, he must seek a remedy before another tribunal.

The case was dismissed, and the warrant was cancelled.

The sequel to the Buonaparte story is short; Captain Burton (in 1861), thinking that the sketch, which was perfect, and the lock of hair which had been preserved in a family watch-case for forty years, would be great treasures to the Buonapartes, and should be given to them, begged the sketch of General and Mrs. Ward, and the hair from the Burtons; he had the hair set in a handsome ring, with a wreath of laurels and the Buonaparte bees. His wife had a complete set of her husband's works very handsomely bound, as a gift, and in January, 1862, Captain Burton sent his wife over to Paris, with the sketch, the ring, and the books, to request an audience with the Emperor and Empress, and offer them these things simply as an act of civility—for Captain and Mrs. Burton are Legitimists. Captain Burton was away on a journey, and Mrs. Burton had to go alone. She was young and inexperienced, had not a single friend in Paris to advise her. She left her letter and presents at the Tuileries. The audience was not granted. His Imperial Majesty declined the presents, and she never heard anything more. Frightened and disappointed at the failure of this, her first little mission at the outset of her married life, she returned to London directly, where she found the Burton family anything but pleased at her failure and her want of *savoir faire* in the matter, having unwittingly caused their treasure to be utterly unappreciated. She said to me on her return, " I never felt so snubbed in my life, and I shall never like Paris again;" and I believe she has kept her word.

OXONIAN.

LIST OF CAPTAIN BURTON'S WORKS.

A Grammar of the Játaki or Belochkí Dialect: Bombay Branch of the Royal Asiatic Society, India, 1849.

Notes on the Pushtú or Afghan Language. Ditto, 1849.

Goa and the Blue Mountains. Bentley, 1851.

Scinde; or The Unhappy Valley. 2 vols., Bentley, 1851.

Sindh, and the Races that Inhabit the Valley of the Indus. Allen, 1851.

Falconry in the Valley of the Indus. Van Voorst, 1852.

A Complete System of Bayonet Exercise. Clowes and Sons, 1853.

Pilgrimage to Meccah and El Medinah. 3 vols., Longmans, 1855.

First Footsteps in East Africa. Longmans, 1856.

Lake Regions of Equatorial Africa. 2 vols., Longmans, 1860.

The whole of Vol. XXXIII. of the Royal Geographical Society. Clowes and Sons, 1860.

The City of the Saints (Mormon). Longmans, 1861.

Wanderings in West Africa. 2 vols., Tinsleys, 1863.

Abeokuta and the Cameroons. 2 vols., Tinsleys, 1863.

The Nile Basin. Tinsleys, 1864.

A Mission to the King of Dáhome. 2 vols., Tinsleys, 1864.

Wit and Wisdom from West Africa. Tinsleys, 1865.

The Highlands of the Brazil. 2 vols., Tinsleys, 1869.

Vikram and the Vampire; Hindú Tales. Longmans, 1870.

Paraguay. Tinsleys, 1870.

Proverba Communia Syriaca. Royal Asiatic Society, 1871.

Zanzibar : City, Island, and Coast. 2 vols., Tinsleys, 1872.

Unexplored Syria ; Richard and Isabel Burton. 2 vols., Tinsleys, 1872.

The Lands of the Cazembe, and a small Pamphlet of Supplementary Papers. Royal Geographical Society, 1873.

The Captivity of Hans Stadt. Hakluyt Society, 1874.

Articles on Rome. 2 Papers, Macmillan's Magazine, 1874–5.

The Castellieri of Istria : a Pamphlet. Anthropological Society, 1874.

New System of Sword Exercise ; a Manual. Clowes and Sons, 1875.

Ultima Thule : a Summer in Iceland. 2 vols., Nimmo, 1875.

Gorilla Land ; or, The Cataracts of the Congo. 2 vols , Sampson Low and Co., 1875.

The Long Wall of Salona, and the Ruined Cities of Pharia and Gelsa di Lesina : a Pamphlet. Anthropological Society, 1875.

The Port of Trieste, Ancient and Modern. Journal of the Society of Arts, October 29th and November 5th, 1875.

Gerber's Province of Minas Geraes. Translated and Annotated by R. F. Burton, Royal Geographical Society.

Etruscan Bologna. Smith and Elder, 1876.

Sind Revisited. 2 vols., Bentley, 1877.

The Gold Mines of Midian and the Ruined Midianite Cities. C. Kegan Paul & Co., 1878.

The Land of Midian (Revisited). 2 vols., C. Kegan
Paul & Co., 1879.

Cheap Edition of Meccah and Medinah. William
Mullan & Son, 1879.

In course of preparation :—

Manoel de Moraes, Iraçema, and "The Uruguay"
(translations from the great Brazilian authors), by
Richard and Isabel Burton ; the Secrets of the Sword ;
The Lowlands of the Brazil ; Translation of Camoens ;
Personal Experiences in Syria ; A Book on Istria ;
Slavonic Proverbs; Greek Proverbs; The Gypsies; Dr.
Wetzstein's "Hauran" and Ladislaus Magyar's African
Travels.

Besides which, Captain Burton has written extensively for " Fraser," " Blackwood," and a host of maga-
zines, pamphlets, and periodicals; has lectured in many
lands; has largely contributed to the newspaper Press
in Europe, Asia, Africa, and America (both North
and South), to say nothing of poetry and anonymous
writings.

BOOKS BY ISABEL BURTON.

Inner Life of Syria. 2 vols., C. Kegan Paul and Co.,
1875. Cheap Edition of one Vol., 1879. Of this book
after something like sixty reviews and two or three
leading articles, the following notice has just appeared
in the *Court Circular* :—

"This book has no need of further praise from any re-
viewer. It has passed through its earlier editions
rapidly, and is now issued in a pretty and cheap form.
It is one of the most pleasant books of travel ever
written, but even the fresh charm of its words about men
and places is of less interest than the admirable pleading
which it offers in favour of a great man who has been

shamefully neglected. While circussy heroes are flourish-
ing about all over the country, and gaining manifest
rewards, our English Odysseus is left out in the cold
shade. Were it only that they may read some truth
about Richard Burton, people should look through the
beautiful book which we have noticed."

Some time ago a notice of the same book contained:—"That no notice has ever been taken of his
services in the shape of *honours* surprises, us his friends,
and the public. It must be some unusually powerful
enemy that can bar him out from honours in the face of
the whole world's applause."

Inner Life in Syria. Second Notice. November 9th, 1875.

Another review contained :—

" Yet, strange to say, as we have stated more than
once, the vast and varied services of Captain Burton to
geography and philology, the perils and adventures in the
quest of knowledge and the furtherance of science, which
would have gained another Desdemona the applause and
consent of the Venetian senators, have, although fully
acknowledged from time to time, never met with any
adequate reward. The man of whom England should
not only be proud, but whose genius and acquirements
she should have utilized in her most important Eastern
negotiations—this man, who has Oriental languages and
literatures at his fingers' ends, as no other living European has or probably ever had, and who possesses a
marvellous influence when dealing with Orientals, which
would have made him our best Eastern diplomatist.
Imagine what use Germany, or Russia, or France would
have made of such a man—what honours they would have
heaped upon him ! But it is thus that England generally
treats and rewards her best, and most accomplished,
and devoted servants, whilst she promotes to places of

high trust and confidence shameless and impudent
flatterers and sycophants, who, if the opportunity arises,
bring her into foolish and unnecessary wars, foreign
odium and contempt, and disgrace and discredit of
every kind. It is now some years since we heard Earl
Derby himself, in a speech made in Captain Burton's
honour, declare that he had then accomplished as much
as would render six men great and famous. That this
is true there can be little doubt—that it was sincere at
the time we should be sorry to question—but it has resulted in the mere shelving, without reward, of the 'six
lives in one.' "

A. E. I. (Arabia, Egypt, India), by William Mullan and
Son, 1879.

Lastly, Mrs. Burton is engaged in preparing Captain
Burton's travels and adventures, in a popular form,
as Boy's Christmas Books, to appear annually.

BURTON'S AUTOBIOGRAPHY.

The only scrap of autobiography we have from Burton's pen was written very early in life whilst in India,
and dates thirty years ago. It is so characteristic it
deserves to be perpetuated.

I extract the following few lines from a well known
literary journal as a kind of excuse for venturing, un-
asked, upon a scrap of autobiography. As long as critics
content themselves with bedevilling one's style, discovering
that one's slang is "vulgar," and one's attempts at drollery
"failures," one should, methinks, listen silently to their
ideas of "gentility," and accept their definitions of wit,
reserving one's own opinion upon such subjects. For
the British author in this, our modern day, engages him-

self as Clown in a great pantomime, to be knocked down, and pulled up, slashed, tickled, and buttered *à discrétion* for the benefit of a manual-pleasantry-loving Public. So it would be weakness in him to complain of bruised back, scored elbows, and bumped head.

Besides, the treatment you receive varies prodigiously according to the temper and the manifold influences from without, that operate upon the gentleman that operates upon you. For instance—

" 'Tis a *failure* at being *funny*," says surly Aristarchus, when, for some reason or other, he dislikes you or your publisher.

" It is a *smart* book," opines another, who has no particular reason to be your friend.

" Narrated with *freshness of thought*," declares a third, who takes an honest pride in "giving the devil his due."

" Very *clever*," exclaims the amiable critic, who for some reason or another likes you or your publisher.

"There is *wit* and *humour* in these pages," says the gentleman who has some particular reason to be your friend.

" Evinces considerable *talent*."

And—

"There is *genius* in this book," declare the l ar rities who in any way identify themselves or their nterests with you.

Now for the extract :—

" Mr. Burton was, it appears, stationed for several years in Sind with his regiment, and it is due to him to say that he has set a good example to his fellow-subalterns by pursuing so diligently his inquiries into the language, literature, and customs of the native population by which he was surrounded. We are far from

accepting all his doctrines on questions of Eastern.
policy, especially as regards the treatment of natives ;.
but we are sensible of the value of the additional evidence which he has brought forward on many important
questions. For a young man, he seems to have adopted
some very extreme opinions; and it is perhaps not too
much to say, that the fault from which he has most to
fear, not only as an author, but as an Indian officer, is a
disregard of those well-established rules of moderation
which no one can transgress with impunity."

The greatest difficulty a raw writer on Indian subjects
has to contend with is is a proper comprehension of the
ignorance crasse which besets the mind of the home-
reader and his oracle the critic. What a knowledge these
lines do show of the opportunity for study presented to
the Anglo-Indian subaltern serving with his corps!
Part of the time when I did duty with mine we were
quartered at Ghárrá, a heap of bungalows surrounded by
a wall of milk-bush; on a sandy flat, near a dirty village whose timorous inhabitants shunned us as walking
pestilences. No amount of domiciliary visitings would
have found a single Sindian book in the place, except
the accounts of the native shopkeepers; and, to the best
of my remembrance, there was not a soul who could
make himself intelligible in the common medium of
Indian intercourse—Hindostani. An ensign stationed at
Dover Castle might write " Ellis's Antiquities ;" a *sous-
lieutenant* with his corps at Boulogne might compose the
" Legendaire de la Morinie," but Ghárrá was sufficient to
paralyse the readiest pen that ever coursed over foolscap
paper.

Now, waiving, with all due modesty, the unmerited
compliment of " good boy," so gracefully tendered to
me, I proceed to the judgment which follows it, my im-

minent peril of "extreme opinions." If there be any value in the "additional evidence" I have "brought forward on important questions," the reader may, perchance, be curious to know how that evidence was collected. So, without further apology, I plunge into the subject.

After some years of careful training for the Church in the north and south of France, Florence, Naples, and the University of Pisa, I found myself one day walking the High Street, Oxford, with all the emotions which a Parisian exquisite of the first water would experience on awaking—at 3 P.M.,—in "Dandakaran's tangled wood."

To be brief, my "college career" was highly unsatisfactory. I began a "reading man," worked regularly twelve hours a day, failed in everything—chiefly, I flattered myself, because Latin hexameters and Greek iambics had not entered into the list of my studies—threw up the classics, and returned to old habits of fencing, boxing, and single-stick, handling the "ribbons," and sketching facetiously, though not wisely, the reverend features and figures of certain half-reformed monks, calling themselves "fellows." My reading also ran into bad courses—Erpenius, Zadkiel, Falconry, Cornelius, Agrippa, and the Art of Pluck.

At last the Afghan War broke out. After begging the paternal authority in vain for the Austrian service, the Swiss Guards at Naples, and even the *Légion étrangère*, I determined to leave Oxford, *coûte qui coûte*. The testy old lady, Alma Mater, was easily persuaded to consign, for a time, to "country nursing" the froward brat who showed not a whit of filial regard for her. So, after two years, I left Trinity without a "little go" in a high dog-cart,—a companion in misfortune too-tooing lustily through a " yard of tin," as the dons started up from their game of bowls to witness the departure of the forbidden vehicle. Thus having thoroughly established the fact that I was fit for nothing but to be " shot at for sixpence a day," and as those Affghans (how I blessed their name !) had cut gaps in many a regiment, my father provided me with a commission in the Indian army, and started me as quickly as feasible for the " land of the sun."

So, my friends and fellow-soldiers, I may address you in the words of the witty thief,—slightly altered from Gil Blas,—" Blessings on the dainty pow of the old dame who turned me out of her house ; for had she shown clemency I should now doubtless be a dyspeptic Don, instead of which I have the honour to be a lieutenant, your comrade."

As the Bombay pilot sprang on board, twenty mouths agape over the gangway, all asked one and the same question. Alas! the answer was a sad one!—the Affghans had been defeated—the avenging army had retreated ! The twenty mouths all ejaculated a something unfit for ears polite.

To a mind thoroughly impressed with the sentiment that

> "Man wants but little here below,
> Nor wants that little long,"

the position of an ensign in the Hon. E. I. Company's Service is a very satisfactory one. He has a horse or two, part of a house, a pleasant mess, plenty of pale ale, as much shooting as he can manage, and an occasional invitation to a dance, where there are thirty-two cavaliers to three dames, or to a dinner-party when a chair unexpectedly falls vacant. But some are vain enough to want more, and of these fools was I.

G

In India two roads lead to preferment. The direct highway is "service;"—getting a flesh wound, cutting down a few of the enemy, and doing something eccentric, so that your name may creep into a despatch. The other path, study of the languages, is a rugged and tortuous one, still you have only to plod steadily along its length, and, sooner or later, you must come to a "staff appointment." *Bien entendu*, I suppose you to be destitute of or deficient in interest whose magic influence sets you down at once, a heaven-born Staff Officer, at the goal which others must toil to reach.

A dozen lessons from Professor Forbes and a native servant on board the *John Knox* enabled me to land with *éclat* as a griff, and to astonish the throng of palanquin bearers that jostled, pushed, and pulled me at the pier head, with the vivacity and nervousness of my phraseology. And I spent the first evening in company with one Dossabhoee Sorabjee, a white-bearded Parsee, who, in his quality of language-master, had vernacularized the tongues of Hormuzd knows how many generations of Anglo-Indian subalterns.

The corps to which I was appointed was then in country quarters at Baroda, in the land of Guzerat; the journey was a long one, the difficulty of finding good instructors there was great, so was the expense, moreover fevers abounded; and, lastly, it was not so easy to obtain leave of absence to visit the Presidency, where candidates for the honours of language are examined. These were serious obstacles to success; they were surmounted, however, in six months, at the end of which time I found myself in the novel position of "passed interpreter in Hindostani."

My success—for I had distanced a field of eleven—encouraged me to a second attempt, and though I had to front all the difficulties over again, in four months my name appeared in orders as qualified to interpret in the Guzerattee tongue.

Meanwhile the Ameers of Sind had exchanged their palaces at Hyderabad for other quarters not quite so comfortable at Hazareebagh, and we were ordered up to the Indus for the pleasant purpose of acting police there. Knowing the Conqueror's chief want, a man who could speak a word of his pet conquests' vernacular dialect, I had not been a week at Kurrachee before I found a language-master and a book. But the study was undertaken *invitâ minervâ*. We were quartered in tents, duststorms howled over us daily, drills and brigade parades were never ending, and, as I was acting interpreter to my regiment, courts-martial of dreary length occupied the best part of my time. Besides, it was impossible to work in such an atmosphere of discontent. The seniors abhorred the barren desolate spot, with all its inglorious perils of fever, spleen, dysentery, and congestion of the brain, the juniors grumbled in sympathy, and the Staff officers, ordered up to rejoin the corps—it was on field service—complained bitterly of having to quit their comfortable appointments in more favoured lands without even a campaign in prospect. So when, a month or two after landing in the country, we were transferred from Kurrachee to Ghárrá—purgatory to the other locale—I threw aside Sindí for Maharatte, hoping, by dint of reiterated examinations, to escape the place of torment as soon as possible. It was very like studying Russian in an English country town; however, with the assistance of Molesworth's excellent dictionary, and the regimental Pundit, or schoolmaster, I gained some knowledge of the dialect, and proved myself duly qualified in it at Bombay. At the same time a brother subaltern and I had jointly leased a Persian Moonshee, one Mirza Mohammed Hosayn, of Shiraz. Poor fellow, after passing through the fires of Sind unscathed, he returned to his delightful land for a few weeks, to die there!—and we laid the foundation of a lengthened course of reading in that most elegant of Oriental languages.

Now it is a known fact that a good Staff appointment has the general effect of doing away with one's bad opinion of any place whatever. So when, by the kindness of a friend whose name *his* modesty prevents my mentioning, the Governor of Sind was persuaded to give me the temporary appointment of Assistant in the Survey, I began to look with interest upon the desolation around me. The country was a new one, so was its population, so was their language. After reading all the works published upon the subject, I felt convinced that none but Mr. Crow and Capt. J. McMurdo had dipped beneath the superficies of things. My new duties compelled me to spend the cold season in wandering over the districts, levelling the beds of canals, and making preparatory sketches for a grand survey. I was thrown so entirely amongst the people as to depend upon them for society, and the "dignity," not to mention the increased allowances of a staff officer, enabled me to collect a fair stock of books, and to gather around me those who could make them of any use. So, after the first year, when I had Persian at my fingers' ends, sufficient Arabic to read, write, and converse fluently, and a superficial knowledge of that dialect of Punjaubee which is spoken in the wilder parts of the province, I began the systematic study of the Sindian people, their manners and their tongue.

The first difficulty was to pass for an Oriental, and this was as necessary as it was difficult. The European official in India seldom, if ever, sees anything in its real light, so dense is the veil which the fearfulness, the duplicity, the prejudice, and the superstitions of the natives hang before his eyes. And the white man lives a life so distinct from the black, that hundreds of the former serve through what they call their "term of exile" without once being present at a circumcision feast, a wedding, or a funeral. More especially the present generation, whom the habit and the means of taking furloughs, the increased facility for enjoying ladies' society, and, if truth be spoken, a greater regard for appearances, if not a stricter code of morality, estrange from their dusky fellow subjects every day and day the more. After trying several characters, the easiest to be assumed was, I found, that of a half Arab, half Iranian, such as may be met with in thousands along the northern shore of the Persian Gulf. The Sindians would have detected in a moment the difference between my articulation and their own, had I attempted to speak their vernacular dialect, but they attributed the accent to my strange country, as naturally as a home-bred Englisman would account for the bad pronunciation of a foreigner calling himself partly Spanish, partly Portuguese. Besides, I knew the countries along the Gulf by heart from books, I had a fair knwledge of the Shiah form of worship prevalent in Persia, and my poor Moonshee was generally at hand to support me in times of difficulty, so that the danger of being detected—even by a "real Simon Pure" —was a very inconsiderable one.

With hair falling upon his shoulders, a long beard, face and hands, arms and feet, stained with a thin coat of henna, Mirza Abdullah of Bushire—your humble servant—set out upon many and many a trip. He was a Bazzaz, a vender of fine linen, calicoes, and muslins—

such chapmen are sometimes admitted to display their wares, even in the sacred harem, by "fast" and fashionable dames—and he had a little pack of *bijouterie* and *virtù* reserved for emergencies. It was only, however, when absolutely necessary that he displayed his stock-in-trade ; generally, he contented himself with alluding to it on all possible occasions, boasting largely of his traffic, and asking a thousand questions concerning the state of the market. Thus he could walk into most men's houses, quite without ceremony ; even if the master dreamed of kicking him out, the mistress was sure to oppose such measure with might and main. He secured numberless invitations, was proposed to by several papas, and won, or had to think he won, a few hearts ; for he came as a rich man and he stayed with dignity, and he departed exacting all the honours. When wending his ways he usually urged a return of visit in the morning, but he was seldom to be found at the caravanserai he specified—was Mirza Abdullah the Bushiri.

The timid villagers collected in crowds to see the rich merchant in Oriental dress, riding spear in hand, and pistols in holsters, towards the little encampment pitched near their settlements. But regularly every evening on the line of march the Mirza issued from his tent and wandered amongst them, collecting much information and dealing out more concerning an ideal master—the Feringhee supposed to be sitting in state amongst the Moonshees, the Scribes, the servants, the wheels, the chains, the telescopes, and the other magical inplements in which the camp abounded. When travelling, the Mirza became this mysterious person's factotum, and often had he to answer the question how much his perquisites and illicit gains amounted to in the course of the year.

When the Mirza arrived at a strange town, his first
step was to secure a house in or near the bazaar, for the
purpose of evening *conversazioni*. Now and then he
rented a shop, and furnished it with clammy dates, viscid
molasses, tobacco, ginger, rancid oil, and strong-smelling
sweetmeats; and wonderful tales Fame told about these
establishments. Yet somehow or other, though they
were more crowded than a first-rate milliner's rooms in
Town, they throve not in a pecuniary point of view;
the cause of which was, I believe, that the polite Mirza
was in the habit of giving the heaviest possible weight
for their money to all the ladies, particularly the pretty
ones, that honourrd him by patronizing his concern.

Sometimes the Mirza passed the evening in a Mosque
listening to the ragged students who, stretched at full
length with their stomachs on the dusty floor, and their
arms supporting their heads, mumbled out Arabic from
the thumbed, soiled, and tattered pages of theology
upon which a dim oil light shed its scanty ray, or he sat
debating the niceties of faith with thé long-bearded,
shaven-pated, blear-eyed, and stolid faced *genius loci*, the
Mullah. At other times, when in merrier mood, he
entered uninvited the first door whence issued the
sounds of music and the dance;—a clean turban and a
polite bow are the best "tickets for soup" the East
knows. Or he played chess with some native friend, or
he consorted with the hemp-drinkers and opium-eaters
in the *estaminets*, or he visited the Mrs. Gadabouts and
Go-betweens who make matches amongst the Faithful,
and gathered from them a precious budget of private
history and domestic scandal.

What scenes he saw! what adventures he went
through! But who would believe, even if he ventured
to detail them?

The Mirza's favourite school for study was the house of an elderly matron on the banks of the Fulailee River, about a mile from the Fort of Hyderabad. Khanum Jan had been a beauty in her youth, and the tender passion had been hard upon her, at least judging from the fact that she had fled her home, her husband, and her native town, Candahar, in company with Mohammed Bakhsh, a purblind old tailor, the object of her warmest affections.

"Ah, he is a regular old hyæna now," would the Joan exclaim in her outlandish Persian, pointing to the venerable Darby as he sat at squat in the cool shade, nodding his head and winking his eyes over a pair of pantaloons which took him a month to sew, "but you should have seen him fifteen years ago, what a wonderful youth he was!"

The knowledge of one mind is that of a million—after a fashion. I addressed myself particularly to that of "Darby;" and many an hour of tough thought it took me before I had mastered its truly Oriental peculiarities, its regular irregularities of deduction, and its strange monotonous one-idea'dness.

Khanum Jan's house was a mud edifice occupying one side of a square formed by tall, thin, crumbling mud walls. The respectable matron's peculiar vanity was to lend a helping hand in all manner of *affaires du cœur*. So it often happened that Mirza Abdullah was turned out of the house to pass a few hours in the garden. There he sat upon his felt rug spread beneath a shadowy tamarind, with beds of sweet-smelling basil around him, his eyes roving over the broad river that coursed rapidly between its wooded banks and the groups gathered at the frequent ferries, whilst the soft strains of mysterious, philosophical, transcendental Hafiz were sounded in his

ears by the other Meerza, his companion, Mohammed
Hosayn—peace be upon him!

Of all economical studies this course was the cheapest.
For tobacco daily, for frequent draughts of milk, for
hemp occasionally, for the benefit of Khanum Jan's
experience, for four months' lectures from Mohammed
Bakhsh, and for sundry other little indulgences, the
Mirza paid, it is calculated, the sum of six shillings.
When he left Hyderabad, he gave a silver talisman to
the dame, and a cloth coat to her protector : long may
they live to wear them!

*   *   *   *   *

Thus it was I formed my estimate of the native character. I am as ready to reform it when a man of more
extensive experience and greater knowledge of the subject will kindly show me how far it transgresses the
well-established limits of moderation. As yet I hold, by
way of general rule, that the Eastern mind—I talk of
the nations known to me by personal experience—is
always in extremes ; that it ignores what is meant by
"golden mean," and that it delights to range in flights
limited only by the *ne plus ultra* of Nature herself.
Under which conviction I am open to correction.

RICHARD F. BURTON.

www.ingramcontent.com/pod-product-compliance
Lightning Source LLC
Chambersburg PA
CBHW020040030726
47499CB00007B/2515